The
Takula
Tree

Westminster Press Books by
ELIZABETH P. FLEMING

Gift from the Mikado
Redcloud & Co.
The Spell on the Stones
The Merry Adventures of
Robin Hood Harlan
The Takula Tree

The
Takula
Tree

By

ELIZABETH P. FLEMING

Illustrated by

ROBERT JEFFERSON

THE WESTMINSTER PRESS

Philadelphia

LIBRARY OF CONGRESS CATALOG CARD NO. 64–10518

PUBLISHED BY THE WESTMINSTER PRESS®

PHILADELPHIA, PENNSYLVANIA, 19107

PRINTED IN THE UNITED STATES OF AMERICA

To Edith

Chapter

1

THE rainy season was over. High on the African plateau the sun shone warm, but there was a pleasant breeze stirring. The elephant grass, still laden with moisture, dripped on the two boys and the dog who were making their way through it. The older boy walked ahead, striking out with his arms and legs to beat down the grass that stood taller than his head.

"See, Paul," he said, shaking the water from his dark face, "I'm Daniel, the dew dryer."

"Dew dryer?" asked Paul, who was as fair as his friend was dark. "That's a new one to me."

"A dew dryer," said Daniel, "is the man who walks ahead and beats down the elephant grass so that the rich white man won't get wet. Dew dryers make a lot of money, sometimes even enough to buy a wife."

"I'll try it too," said Paul and started thrashing his arms and legs as he had seen Daniel do. But it was hard work, and with every step a shower of icy water poured down on his head.

"I give up," he said. "I don't want a wife anyway."

Daniel laughed. "We're almost where I wanted to take you," he said. "There's the takula tree."

The tree stood tall and beautiful against the blue sky, a landmark in the field of grass. The boys walked faster, and the dog that had been ranging back and forth, now dashing after some animal in the grass, now following at a distance, fell in close behind them.

"What's so special about this place?" asked Paul.

"Wait and see," said Daniel.

Paul grinned. A walk with Daniel was always worthwhile, for Daniel knew all sorts of queer places to go, and he had a story to tell about each one of them. He knew the names of all the animals and how they lived and what his people believed about them. Paul never tired of listening to him.

"This used to be lion country," said Daniel, "but not anymore. I wish there were lions. I chose Daniel for my Christian name because he made friends with the lions. I'd like to do that too. Of course there are plenty of other animals," he went on. "Antelopes and zebras, giraffes and wild pigs."

"And leopards," said Paul.

"Not many leopards. Someday I'll tell you the story of the leopard and the hare, but

8

here we are at the takula tree. Do you think you could find your way here by yourself?"

Paul glanced at him in surprise. Daniel was looking at him seriously. He was waiting for an answer. "Well, I suppose so," said Paul uncertainly. "But why would I want to come here by myself?"

Daniel didn't answer at once. He pointed to what seemed to be a mound of vines and bushes. "This is the place I wanted you to see," he said.

When Paul came closer he saw that it was a low thatched hut, overgrown with vegetation. "No one lives here?" he asked.

"Not anymore," said Daniel. "It used to be my uncle's forge. He was a metalworker and so was his father before him. It used to be a fine thing to be a metalworker, but that's all over with. People say that now they can buy better hoes and rakes and axes at the store. This place has been empty and forgotten for a long time. It's a very good place to hide."

"But who wants to hide?"

"Maybe you will and your father and mother," said Daniel.

"You must be fooling," Paul answered. He look anxiously at his friend, expecting him to smile. But Daniel's face was sober.

"Haven't you heard the drums at night?" Daniel asked. "They're not beating for fun. The man Yona has come back from the north and is talking about independence. He's stirring up

9

bad trouble. There are plenty who want to drive out the white man. If Yona has his way, that's what they'll try to do, and then the white settlers will put them down with a vengeance and all the rest of us will suffer too. There's going to be terrible trouble. If things get too bad, you must bring your father and mother here. You do understand, don't you?"

Paul felt a coldness at the back of his neck. Could Daniel really mean it? Maybe it was just talk. But Daniel was waiting for an answer. "I—I guess so," Paul stammered.

Daniel seemed satisfied for the time being anyway. He was parting the vines that covered the door of the hut. "Come in," he invited and stepped inside.

The hut was small, but it had a steep roof, high enough for a tall man to stand upright. It was quite dark, but as Paul's eyes got used to it, he could see in the middle of the dirt floor a fire pit with charcoal still in it. Three stone seats were set around the hearth.

"The benches were for the blacksmith's helpers," explained Daniel. "They worked the bellows to make the fire hot. The iron had to be red hot before the master smith could hammer it into shape on the anvil." He was looking around proudly as he spoke.

"It's a nice place," said Paul politely. But he was thinking that anyone would be crazy to leave the comfortable mission house to live in a place like this.

"The anvils are outside under the tree," said Daniel. "I'll show them to you." He parted the grass outside and uncovered a big, flat stone set up on some rocks. Nearby there was a smaller one just like it. "The big anvil was for the master, and the little one for the learner," Daniel explained. "It was a great thing to be a metalworker in the old days. People thought they used magic to make their tools. Everyone looked up to them. My grandfather trained his son in all the secrets of metalworking," he went on. "When he was ready he had to take an examination."

"Examinations aren't much fun," said Paul. His father was principal of the mission school. He knew how everyone worried over examinations.

"No," said Daniel, "it wasn't fun. My grandfather was a hard master. But at last when he was satisfied he invited all the village to come and watch him make a hammer that would be the badge of the new master metalworker. My grandfather heated the iron and beat it on the anvil while everyone looked on, and all the while he was doing it, his son stood on the small anvil and never said a word. Like this," said Daniel and jumped on the small anvil, where he stood with folded arms and stared straight

11

ahead. "When the hammer was finished," he went on, "my grandfather turned to his son. 'You may speak,' he said. 'What name have you chosen for yourself now that you are a master metalworker?'

"'I am Hosi, the lion,' shouted my uncle, and he jumped down from the anvil, and everyone clapped and made trilling noises with their fingers in their mouths. Like this," said Daniel, and jumped down, trilling loudly.

"Hurray," shouted Paul and did his best to trill too, while the dog, who had been watching, barked with all his might.

"Good dog," said Paul. "Good old Ombua."

"Ombua will help you find this place," Daniel told him, coming back to the subject again.

"I wish you wouldn't talk that way," said Paul. "This is a very nice place, but isn't it kind of lonely? Is that why your uncle doesn't live here anymore?"

"My uncle has to work on the Quadros plantation," said Daniel. "There's no work at the forge, and the Government makes men work wherever they're needed, whether the men want to or not. That Quadros is a bad man," he ended bitterly. "It's men like Quadros who start all the trouble."

Paul stirred uncomfortably. Quadros was white and Paul was too. Sometimes people seemed to think that the same color made peo-

12

ple alike. It wasn't true, of course. Quadros wasn't a bit like Mr. and Mrs. Manship, Paul's father and mother.

"All the men who work for Quadros hate him," said Daniel. "They're the ones who listen to Yona's talk. But Matthew is listening too," he added. "He believes everything Yona tells him."

"Not Matthew," cried Paul. Matthew was one of the best students in the mission school. He was graduating with honors the very next day. Paul and Daniel, who were younger, had always looked up to him. Whenever he noticed them, they were pleased and proud. Sometimes Matthew condescended to give them honey from his bee tree, and once he had given Paul a baby rabbit. It grew up and went back to the woods, but Paul had never forgotten the giver.

"Not Matthew," he said again, shocked at the very idea.

"Matthew is smarter than anyone else," said Daniel. "He thinks he knows everything. You never can tell which way he'll jump. Yona is telling him he'll be a leader when independence comes. He doesn't know enough to see it's only talk. You'd better tell your father about it. If the Government finds out, it will make big trouble for the mission." He stood up. "I must be going. Now that the rains are over, there's work I have to do in the fields. I don't mind telling you," he grinned, "the hoe your father gave me

13

is better than one my uncle Hosi could make."

Paul whistled to his dog and the boys started back the way they had come. "Tomorrow is commencement and the picnic," said Paul. "The hunters brought in an antelope yesterday. Everything is about ready."

"What is a 'pick nick'?" asked Daniel, pronouncing the word carefully.

"I've never been to one," Paul confessed, "but they have picnics in America when people graduate from school. My mother and father say it'll be a good thing to have before the graduates go off to start their bush schools."

"If all white people were like Mr. and Mrs. Manship, no one would ever listen to Yona," said Daniel. "What's that?" he raised his head. Farther over in the tall grass a man's voice was raised in a wild chant.

"White ant, white ant," he shouted. "You who are in the way, get out!"

"It's Yona," whispered Daniel. "Don't let him see you."

They crouched in the grass, Daniel's hand on Ombua's collar to quiet him. The voice came nearer. Over the top of the high grass the boys could see a man's head and shoulders. He had a companion, a handsome boy with a proud lift to his head. His voice, high and wild, mounted over the other's in an obbligato. "White ant," he sang, "you who are in my way, get out!"

14

"It's Matthew," said Paul in a shocked whisper.

The singers passed close, but the boys were well hidden. They crouched where they were a little longer, then Paul drew a breath. "Does he mean that we're like white ants?" he asked.

Daniel looked sober. "You see why I want you to remember the forge," he said.

"But everyone has always been so nice to me," Paul stated.

"I know," Daniel replied. "But just remember the takula tree, will you?"

After that, they walked on in silence. When they came to the path that led to the village, Daniel turned aside. "Don't forget," he said again.

There was a hedge around the mission compound, with a gate at the front and one at the back. Paul went in the back way, where Ngonga, the man of all work, was sweeping the yard with a broom of twigs.

"Did you hear the drums?" asked Ngonga. "That Yona's trying to stir up trouble. He's talking all the time about independence. He says that when we get it, every man will have a jeep of his own and a fine house, like the white man." He lowered his voice. "Matthew has been listening to Yona. That boy, Matthew, is too smart for his own good. He thinks he's ready to be the governor or something. You'd better tell your father about it right away. His mother, Vitundo, can't do a thing with him."

Paul's mother was at the door. "Oh, there you are," she called. "Dinner's almost ready."

Paul's father was in the study signing diplomas, and his mother was loading her Polaroid camera. "We'll have pictures this year," she said happily. "I'll snap the pictures as the graduates get their diplomas. They'll be looking their very best then. I do believe the pictures are the crowning point of the whole day."

"It's a good class," said Mr. Manship, "the best we've ever had. Every one of the students deserves to go on to the Government school, but only one's to be accepted." He sighed.

"What reason do they give this time for not taking more?" asked his wife.

"The same old reason. Education will unfit the African to take the place the white man wants to keep him in."

"The very idea," cried Mrs. Manship indignantly. "But I suppose we should be glad that even one is to have a chance. Which one will it be?"

"Matthew is our brightest boy," said Mr. Manship.

Mrs. Manship looked doubtful. "He's the brightest, but do you think he can be trusted on his own?"

"It's a question," said Mr. Manship, "but it

17

wouldn't be fair not to give him his chance. There's no one to compare with him in the whole school except Daniel, of course, who's still too young."

"Matthew's been listening to Yona's talk about independence," Paul put in.

"Where did you hear that?" asked his father, startled.

"Daniel told me and Ngonga too, but I saw him myself going through the tall grass with Yona and singing a song about 'white ant, get out.' He means us, doesn't he? Yona says everyone's going to have a jeep and a fine house when they get independence."

"Oh, this is too bad," cried Mr. Manship.

"And Matthew believes that!" cried Mrs. Manship. "That's what I mean. He's a smart boy, but he hasn't good common sense. He ought to know that there can't be independence until there are educated men to take over, and there are no educated men because the Government won't let the Africans go to school."

"People don't like us very well," said Paul.

"Oh, yes they do," said his mother perhaps a little too quickly. "They all know that we at the mission want the very best for them. It's people like Mr. Quadros, who treats his men so badly, that they mean."

"They have reason to be angry," said Mr. Manship sadly.

Esther, the mission helper, stood in the door-
18

way. "Excuse me," she said and slipped across the room to where the trash container stood beside Mr. Manship's desk. It was a bright blue with white lettering on its front. "Tip-top," it said. Esther knelt and with one hand gently pressed the lever. The top flew up, and she took some scraps of paper from inside and went quietly away.

Mr. and Mrs. Manship smiled at each other. They knew how Esther felt about the tip-top. It had come from America along with the new refrigerator, a gift from some kind friend, and Esther had fallen in love with it. "Magic," she cried when the cover flew up in her astonished face.

"It's a nice garbage pail, isn't it?" said Mrs. Manship.

Esther was horrified. "We have the Standard Oil can for garbage," she cried. "This magic box is too beautiful for such a use."

"We can use it for the kitchen wastebasket," Mrs. Manship told her.

"Not the kitchen wastebasket," said Esther. "Too many people come and go in the kitchen. Mr. Manship's study is the only safe place for it."

It was true that the study was the only room in the house where no one could go without permission. So the tip-top became the study wastebasket, carefully watched over by Esther, and emptied many times a day.

19

"I always feel a little guilty about using it," said Mr. Manship.

"But think how disappointed Esther would be if she couldn't empty it," smiled Mrs. Manship.

Esther had come to the mission, a hungry, frightened little girl and had remained to be the mainstay of the whole place. "I do believe Esther could run this place single-handed," Mrs. Manship often said. If anything needed doing, Esther was always ready to do it. She knew everything that went on over the whole countryside and never refused help or encouragement.

"Esther, what about this man Yona?" Mr. Manship asked as they sat down to dinner.

"Yona is a very bad man," Esther told him. "He killed a man a long time ago and then he ran away. Now he thinks that it's forgotten and he has come back to stir up trouble. He wants to kill all the white men and get independence. He's promising all kinds of things to men who follow him. First thing we know, there's going to be bad trouble."

"But if he's a murderer, won't they put him in jail?" asked Mrs. Manship.

"They couldn't catch him," said Esther. "He knows all the secret ways through the bush. Five hundred men could be looking for him and never find him. He's too smart. And another thing, Mr. Manship, I hate to tell you, but

20

Matthew is all carried away by Yona's talk. He thinks he's going to be something big when independence comes. He's following Yona around like a little dog."

Mr. Manship shook his head. "I'll have to have a talk with him. It looks as though we'll have to have second thoughts about his going to the Government school," he added sadly.

"Do you think Yona can get much of a following?" asked Mrs. Manship anxiously.

Mr. Manship shook his head. "As far as our people go, they'd never be led astray by him. Matthew's young and his head has been turned with flattery. For ten years we have preached forbearance and nonresistance. They know it's the only Christian way. They won't be tempted to violence."

"Daniel says it's the men who work on the Quadros plantation," said Paul. "They don't want to work there and the Government makes them and they don't get enough pay, and they hate Quadros."

"They have their grievances," said Mr. Manship. "Sometimes I feel that it's more than flesh and blood can bear to keep silent. But if I speak, I'll be deported. The Government is wrong, wrong, wrong. But these poor ignorant men can't do anything against the ruling class. No, I don't think there'll be any trouble yet. Later, who knows?"

Paul had almost forgotten about the little

forge and what Daniel had said about its being a good place to hide. Well, no matter. His father said there wasn't going to be any trouble, and back here at the mission the thought of having to hide in the forge seemed silly. Daniel was smart, but he was only a boy. Grown-ups, especially Paul's father, knew best. Paul was hungry. The dinner tasted very good, but antelope roasted whole for the picnic would taste even better. He forgot all about Yona and Matthew and the little forge in lovely thoughts of tomorrow.

Chapter

2

THE mission hall rocked with excitement. Commencement was in full swing. Mr. Manship had been speaking to the graduates about the danger of listening to the people who talked of violence.

"Violence is never the Christian way," he said. "No good can come of it. Remember, graduates, that teaching in your bush schools is the surest way to help your people. Education must come before independence. So go, my friends, to your schools with love and charity for all. And may God bless you in your work."

It was time to give out the diplomas. As each graduate's name was called, he stepped forward to receive his diploma and posed with smiling face to have his picture taken. Many of the graduates were married; some had children. Wives and children watched breathlessly until Mrs. Manship's camera clicked, then they burst into applause and giggles. Everyone was happy. After the exercises would come the picnic. No one had even been to a picnic and that made it all the better. The fine, fat antelope brought in by the hunters was already roasting, and the good smell drifted through the windows.

"Matthew Jamba," Mr. Manship called the name, and Matthew, swaggering a little, made his way to the platform. Matthew was young; he had no wife. Only his mother, Vitundo, was there to clap for him. He struck a defiant pose as his picture was taken and went back to his seat with his head in the air. There was very little applause. No one approved of his friendship with Yona. They sat silent. Paul, remembering the honey and the rabbit, did his best, and Daniel joined him, but it was only a spattering that soon died out.

I must have a talk with Matthew, Mr. Manship said to himself. Aloud he called out, "Joseph Katito," the name of the next graduate. There was no answer, but a small boy stood up.

"Joseph is sick," he piped.

There was a wail from the back of the hall and Ndumbila, Joseph's wife, rushed to the platform. "Joseph is dying," she cried.

At the words, all happiness seemed to flee. Sighs and groans took the place of laughter. "Ah, poor Joseph," they groaned. "Poor Joseph."

Mr. Manship tried to cheer them. "I'm sure it's not that bad," he said. "I'll go to Joseph, but the exercises will continue. Daniel will read off the names in my place, and Mrs. Manship will give out the diplomas and take the pictures as she has been doing. And, remember the picnic afterward," he added cheerfully.

They were reassured. Daniel, though he was young, was the finest student in the school. It was right that he should help Mrs. Manship. Bashfully Daniel stepped forward. "Mark Manu," he called out in a good, loud voice. The commencement exercises went forward without a hitch.

Mr. Manship slipped quietly out of the door and hurried after the frightened Ndumbila, who was running back to the village. He found Joseph lying in his dark little hut, surrounded by a circle of women who crouched on the ground, moaning in sympathy.

"Commencement," cried Joseph, trying to sit up when he saw Mr. Manship. "Without commencement I am nothing." The sweat was running down his face. He could scarcely keep back his groans of pain.

"You're a graduate just the same," soothed Mr. Manship. "You've earned your diploma. Don't worry about that. Where do you have pain?" He was pressing gently on Joseph as he murmured words of encouragement. "I think we'd better get you to the hospital as soon as we can," he said after a minute. "They'll fix you up there."

25

The hospital! At the word poor Ndumbila set up a wail and her friends joined in. The little hut shook with their cries.

"Now, now," said Mr. Manship, "you'll disturb Joseph's spirit. The hospital is the place to get him well. Ndumbila, get some things together for the journey, and I'll bring the jeep right to the door to get him."

No one moved. It was almost as though he had not spoken. The women kept on weeping and wailing. He could never manage them by himself. The only thing to do was to go to the mission for help. He hurried back the way he had come. The exercises were over and the company was out in the mission yard singing.

"I'm afraid it's appendicitis," Mr. Manship whispered to his wife. "I'll have to get him to the hospital as soon as possible. Ndumbila and her friends seem to have lost their wits. They do nothing but cry. Do you think you could go down there and straighten things out while I get the jeep?"

Mrs. Manship looked at the crowd in the yard. "How can I?" she asked.

Esther came over to them. "I'll go," she volunteered.

"Oh, Esther," said Mrs. Manship, "what would we do without you?"

"I hate to leave you alone when Yona's trying to stir up trouble," said Mr. Manship with a worried face.

26

"Yona won't bother us," said Mrs. Manship. "And you won't be gone long."

"Not any longer than I can help. I should be back tomorrow night, that is, if the roads aren't too bad." He broke off with a frown. They both knew that after the rains the roads would be a sea of mud. Even a jeep would not find it easy going.

"Esther and Paul and I can take care of ourselves," said Mrs. Manship. "And we have Ngonga too," she added.

"I'm depending on you to take care of things," Mr. Manship turned to Ngonga, who smiled proudly at the trust. Ngonga was willing and faithful. Nothing could go wrong over one night, Mr. Manship told himself.

When Esther reached Joseph's hut she found the women still sitting on the floor. "Ndumbila, get up," she said. "Go out and catch a chicken to pay the white doctor for getting Joseph well. The rest of you bring blankets and food for the journey to the hospital." She spoke as though she expected them to do what she said, and they scattered without a word. "Joseph," she said softly, "don't be afraid. The white doctor will soon make you well." She wiped his face with a cool, damp cloth and straightened his bed, so that he was more comfortable.

One by one the women came back with blankets, a clean shirt for Joseph, bread, and sweet potatoes. "Who will go to nurse Joseph?"

27

asked Esther. "Ndumbila, of course, though she won't be much good. Evova, Joseph's mother's brother, and his wife—" she hesitated.

"I will go," said Ndumbila's sister, a young woman with a baby astride one hip.

"And I," said Nogo, her eyes shining at the thought of a ride in the jeep. Nogo was Ngonga's young wife, very pert and pretty, with never a thought of anything but herself.

Esther looked at her disapprovingly. "You have no kinship with Joseph," she said.

At her words the others gave a cackle of laughter. They knew Nogo. She had no idea of nursing Joseph. It was only the trip she wanted. Crossly Nogo turned to go out of the door and everyone drew in a breath of surprise and disapproval. Across the back of her dress something was written in large letters. "INDEPENDENCE," it said. The women could not read, but they knew very well what it meant. Yona had given the dress to Nogo. What was Ngonga thinking of to allow his wife to wear it?

Things were moving too fast for talk. The women rushed in and out in a flutter, and Ndumbila managed to catch a chicken. They were ready when Mr. Manship brought the jeep to the door.

Joseph was lifted carefully to the front seat and the relatives wedged themselves in the back. Everyone else ran alongside to the mission house where Mrs. Manship waited with pillows and blankets to make Joseph as comfortable as possible. Mr. Manship brought a pill to soothe the pain, and Paul was ready with a glass of water to wash it down. The picnickers stood about, full of sympathy, but pleasantly excited too. It wasn't often that any of their number had a chance to ride in the jeep. It was too bad that Joseph was sick, but the white doctor, who knew everything, would soon make him well. There was no need to worry.

"I'll radio as soon as I get there," Mr. Manship was saying to his wife when Nogo came flying down the road.

"Wait! Wait!" she screamed. "Don't take the baby. He's young and tender. The white doctor will eat him instead of the chicken."

A cry of horror rose from the company, and Ndumbila's sister, clutching the baby, stood up and tried to climb out over the relatives.

"Sit down," said Mr. Manship, putting a soothing hand on her shoulder. "Nogo is talking nonsense and knows it. Joseph is a sick man, and we must get him to the hospital as soon as we can, where the white doctor will get him well. Are you ready?" he turned to the others.

"Ready," they cried. They were off in a chorus of good-bys. Even Joseph managed to wave a feeble farewell.

Nogo stood undecided, a frown on her face,

29

but the smell of roasting antelope was too much for her. She slipped into the mission yard to join the others in the picnic.

No antelope was ever browner or crisper, no sweet potatoes better tasting. They ate until they could eat no more. Then a silence fell on the crowd. This was the time when Mr. Manship would have known what to do. But he wasn't there. By themselves they might have danced and sung, but no one was ready to start. What was to be done? Paul saw the worried look on his mother's face and knew he must do something. He hurried to the study and came back with Esther's beloved tip-top.

"Right this way, everybody," he shouted. "Take your places in line for a try at the magic box from America."

Mrs. Manship was smiling, but Esther's face was the picture of distress. "They'll break it," she said.

"No, they won't," Paul reassured her. "You can stand right here and watch them. One chance only," he raised his voice. "One chance at the magic tip-top."

They were laughing as they formed a line. Nogo was in the lead. A murmur of disapproval went up as they saw the word "INDEPENDENCE" on the back of her dress, and Ngonga turned away in confusion. But Nogo was not embarrassed. She was giggling as she crouched in front of the tip-top.

"Easy does it," said Paul. "Put your hand on the black pedal."

Nogo pushed and the cover flew up. With a squeak she fell back, and a roar of laughter went up from the waiting line. "Let me try again," cried Nogo, but Esther shook her head. "One chance only," she said firmly.

Slowly the line moved forward. One by one they pushed the lever cautiously, and each time the cover flew up they were taken unawares, while shouts of laughter burst from the onlookers. They were still laughing when at last they started homeward.

"Three cheers for tip-top," said Paul when he and his mother and Esther stood alone in the mission yard.

"Paul," said his mother, "that was a wonderful idea of yours. I wish the people who gave the tip-top could know what fun everyone had with it."

Esther was going over it with anxious care. "The children have left finger marks on it," she said.

"They'll wash off," said Paul. "It was a dandy picnic, wasn't it? Was it as good as the ones in America, Mother?"

"Better," said his mother, "because in America people have so much, that they're likely to take things for granted. I wish your father could have been here," she went on. "I think he must be almost there by now. Poor Joseph, I hope he

31

stands the trip all right. I'm afraid the roads are very bad."

"Mark told me there has been no work done on the roads since the rains," said Esther. "The women who'd been drafted ran away and hid. Yona sets them up to it."

"I don't like Yona," said Mrs. Manship, "but I hate this idea of women working on the roads. It's a disgrace. The Government has no business to make them."

"The Government!" was all that Esther said, but her voice said a great deal more.

It was getting late. Even with bad roads it seemed that Mr. Manship would call soon. But darkness fell and still there was no radio message. Off in the distance a drum began to beat. It grew louder and louder. There were shouts and snatches of song. "I never get used to the drums," sighed Mrs. Manship.

"They're speaking no good tonight," said Esther.

Mrs. Manship stood up. "Father should be calling soon," she said. "Let's go into the study to be ready."

The radio receiving set was in the corner of the study. "Look, Mother!" gasped Paul and pointed. The set was in ruins. Someone had chopped it to pieces with an ax. They stared at it unbelievingly.

"How could it have happened?" Mrs. Manship began, then she recovered herself. "I sup-

pose someone wanted to know how it worked," she added. "They are always so interested in new things. Like the tip-top garbage pail." Her voice sounded almost natural again.

"But they didn't need to break it," said Paul. He looked up to see Esther's face, and the same cold feeling went down his spine that he had felt when Daniel said the forge would be a good hiding place. He told them about it then. "Daniel took me to the forge that belonged to his mother's brother. Nobody knows about it. We can go there and hide until Dad gets home."

"We don't have to go anywhere," his mother's voice was reassuring. "We're perfectly safe here. It's nothing if the radio doesn't work. It's been out of order before."

Paul was not convinced. "No one smashed it before."

His mother didn't give a direct answer to that. "Dad will be home tomorrow," she said. "I hope he won't worry because he can't get us. But why should he?" she asked brightly. "We're among friends. How proud the graduates were with their diplomas and pictures. And what a good time we had at the picnic." She was especially gay after that, and before bedtime she read aloud for a while, Paul and Esther sitting on either side of her to listen.

Later, when Paul was in bed, the drums seemed to grow louder. His mother and Esther

34

were talking in quiet voices. After a while he heard them locking doors and windows. It was the first time he ever remembered their being locked. The house always stood open for people to come and go as they liked. Of course, he told himself, his father was away and that made the difference. He was tired. Even a vague uneasiness couldn't keep him awake for long. He drifted off to sleep with the sound of drums still in his ears.

. . .

He woke the next morning to sun streaming in the window. The doors were open and breakfast was ready. They had a cheerful meal. "Your father should be home today," his mother remarked. "We'll have a good story to tell him about the picnic."

"The garbage pail was the biggest hit," said Paul.

"I was afraid they'd break it," said Esther, "but it's all right. I washed off the fingerprints. It looks like new."

"Will you get someone to fix the radio today?" Paul wanted to know.

There was a little silence. "Perhaps," said his mother. "But Dad'll be home soon, so it won't make any difference."

"I wish he'd never gone away," said Esther.

"But, Esther, he had to. Joseph might have died," cried Mrs. Manship.

Esther said something under her breath. It

35

sounded like, Maybe we'll die too. Then she spoke out loud. "I don't like the drums."

"I can't see why anyone broke the radio," Paul wondered, going back to the thing that made him uneasy.

"I can't either," said his mother.

He was still thinking about it when something bit his leg. "Ouch!" he cried, catching at the spot. An ant dropped to the floor and scurried away.

"Look!" gasped Mrs. Manship. Ants were coming in the door, a whole army of them. They moved across the floor in a close-packed solid column, with enormous soldier ants rushing up and down the line keeping order. Ombua, who had been asleep on the floor, jumped up with a howl.

"Get up on the chair," ordered Paul. "Good dog, up." He pushed a chair forward and Ombua scrambled up.

"What'll we do?" cried Mrs. Manship, drawing her feet up under her. "Quick, Esther, get the DDT."

"We mustn't try to stop them," said Esther. "See, they're going out of the window."

Sure enough, marshaled by the soldier ants, the column had crossed the room and the leaders were climbing the wall to disappear out of the window. But still they came on, thousands of them in a procession that seemed to have no end.

36

"All we can do is try to keep them away from us," said Esther, laying a circle of DDT around the table where they sat, feet tucked up, watching in horrified fascination.

"Some of them are carrying eggs," said Paul. "And there's a piece of corn bread from the picnic. Look, a beetle." The soldier ants were on the beetle in a minute. He curled up when they stung him. Then a squad of ants separated from the others and carried him off. "I suppose they're going to eat him by and by," said Paul.

Just then Mrs. Manship gave a squeal as a soldier ant dashed through the DDT and up the leg of her chair. "Onto the table," cried Esther, and breathlessly they scrambled to safety. Ombua looked at them forlornly. He was a well-trained dog. He wouldn't jump onto the table without permission.

"Oh, well, come up," said Mrs. Manship, laughing. Ombua jumped up and sat himself down among the dishes. "Of all the ridiculous things," said Mrs. Manship, reaching behind her to stack the breakfast dishes. But Paul was giggling and soon all three of them were laughing helplessly as the ants streamed by.

It couldn't last forever. The line was growing thinner. Finally only a few stragglers were left. Then the last soldier ant disappeared through the window, and it was safe to get down.

"Where are they going?" asked Paul.

"Just moving," Esther told him. "Sometimes they get a notion."

Ngonga came to the door. "Are you all right?" he asked. "I couldn't stop them."

They looked out of the door. A swath had been picked perfectly clean across the length of the yard. "I've heard that ants will do that," said Mrs. Manship, "but I didn't know it was like this."

Esther was washing every crack and corner of the room, and Mrs. Manship followed with the spray. They wanted to be sure no stray ant was left behind. Paul helped at first, but he soon tired of it. The women were so intent on their work that they did not notice when he strolled out of the house. It didn't occur to him that he might be safer at home.

Chapter

3

THERE was no school, and Paul had nothing to do. Ngonga had finished his work and gone away. Ombua, worn out with the ant parade, was sleeping. He opened one eye when Paul spoke to him, but he didn't get up. Paul walked slowly across the courtyard, past the schoolhouse, and let himself out the front gate. The path to the village was muddy, but the sun would soon dry it. On either side the tall elephant grass stirred gently in the breeze. Here on the uplands, though it was near the Equator, the air was cool and pleasant.

The village was a cluster of beehive-shaped mud huts. A few had roofs of rusted corrugated iron, but most of them were thatched with straw. A goat or two and some pigs rooted in the dirt. A few little children played about with an old grandmother to watch them. Paul saw no one else, but the sound of music came to his ears and he followed it. Matthew was sitting in front of his hut playing a tune on a wooden instrument he had made himself. Matthew, thought Paul, is clever about ever so many things.

"Hello," greeted Paul.

Matthew kept right on playing.

"Matthew, hello." Paul raised his voice a little.

Matthew stopped playing. "My name is Jamba," he said.

Paul was taken aback. What could Matthew mean by that? Many of the students took a Bible name when they became Christians. If Matthew was dropping his Christian name, did it mean he was going back to the old ways? Was he giving up the mission?

"Africa for the Africans," said Matthew and went back to his music.

Nogo, Ngonga's wife, who was balancing a basket of sweet potatoes on her head, came out of her hut. When she was quite close to Paul, she stamped her foot. "Ha!" she said.

Paul went hot and cold. Never in all his life had he been treated like that. He stared indignantly after Nogo. Across the back of her dress the word "INDEPENDENCE" stared at him. Maybe it was the dress that made her so stuck-up. He turned back to Matthew, expecting sympathy, but Matthew had resumed playing his music. He acted as though Paul wasn't even there. Hurt and angry, Paul started away.

40

Daniel would be working in the field. He, at least, would be glad to see him.

"Hello," Paul called out as he caught sight of his friend bent over his hoeing. "Want any help around here?"

It was only after he had spoken that he saw that Daniel was not alone. A man squatted at the edge of the field. He rose and stared at Paul, who felt a shiver of fear. The man's face was marked with scars that rayed out from his nose, a dreadful face, sinister and cruel. Of course, Paul knew about those scars. Daniel had told him that in the old days every boy went off into the bush to be initiated. They often cut their faces or their bodies and rubbed in wood ashes so the scars never healed. They didn't do it much anymore, Daniel said, because the Government was against it, but there were still secret initiations in the bush.

The man was coming toward Paul. "White boy," he said, "go home. No one needs your help. Africa for the Africans," his voice rose to a shout. "White ant, *get out!*"

Paul stood his ground. "I'm an African," he said. "Everyone born in Africa is an African. My father says so."

"*Get out!*" the man roared.

Daniel stepped between them. "You'd better go home," he said. Paul could scarcely believe his ears. But Daniel came close to him. "It isn't

41

safe," he whispered. "Yona wants to kill all the white people."

"All right," said Paul, but he wasn't going to hurry. No one was going to say that he ran away. Eyes straight ahead, he walked slowly, though shivers were running up and down his spine. He expected Yona to grab him any minute, but nothing stirred behind him. After a little, he heard the scrape of Daniel's hoe in the dirt. It must be that Yona had decided to leave him alone.

Paul was miserable. All he wanted was to get home, away from everybody. He couldn't go back through the village, for there Matthew and Nogo would see him. Instead, he took the road that led past the Quadros plantation. Men would be working there, but they didn't know him. Perhaps he could hurry past without their noticing. To his surprise the plantation was deserted. No one was at work. He walked slowly, staring at the empty fields. A dark shape was moving between the rows. What was the man up to? As Paul watched curiously, absorbed, someone gave him a violent push from the back and he fell to his knees. There was a shout and a rush of feet, then quiet. Scared and indignant, Paul scrambled to his feet. There was no one in sight. He started onward and suddenly his eye was caught by smoke rising from the field. A flame shot up.

"Fire!" he shouted. He stamped on the flame

42

and it died out only to spring up farther on. Fanned by the wind, it leaped to the next row. "Help!" he shouted. "Help!" Mr. Quadros came running, another man close behind. The three worked together, beating at the flames with leafy branches and stamping them underfoot. It was almost over when Paul heard the scream. A little girl raced toward him, a flame licking at her dress. He yanked off the flimsy garment and trampled it underfoot.

"My dress!" she cried.

"Did you want to get burned up?" he asked.

Quadros' companion caught her up in his arms. "Isobel," he scolded, "what are you doing here? I told you to stay in the house." He was carrying her away, but her voice came back to Paul.

"I was trying to help, Papa," she wailed.

Quadros and Paul were left alone. The fire was out, but Quadros was seething. "The blackguards," he shouted. "They quit work and now they've fired my cotton. I'll have the law on them. I'll shoot them down like dogs." His eyes were bloodshot, his lips curled back from his teeth. Paul backed away from him.

"This is your father's fault," snarled Quadros. "It's these missionaries who are making all the trouble, training terrorists. Tell him to get out. Leave the Africans alone. This is white man's country."

Paul turned and ran. Esther was waiting for

43

him at the mission gate. "Where have you been?" she asked. "Don't you know better than to go wandering off when Yona is stirring up trouble?" She was scolding him, but her arms were tight about him. He could feel that she was trembling.

"We've been worried," cried his mother. "You've been in a fire! Your clothes are scorched!"

They hurried him into the house before he had a chance to tell his story. Esther was shutting doors and windows all the time he was talking.

"Mr. Quadros was mean," Paul said. "He didn't even thank me for helping him put out the fire." He had forgotten all about the girl Isobel and her father. "And he said it was Father's fault that there was trouble. He said, 'Get out,' just the way Yona did."

"He was angry and upset," said Mrs. Manship.

"Yona was with Daniel," Paul went on. "He said, 'White boy, go home.' Daniel told me to go too. He said Yona wants to kill all the white people. And Matthew and Nogo were mean to me. Nobody likes us."

"Oh, yes, they do," said his mother. "The people that count know that we're their friends."

"That Yona is a bad man," said Esther.

"The thing for us to do is to stay right here

44

until your father comes home," said Mrs. Manship. "Paul, you mustn't go out again."

"I don't want to go anywhere," said Paul. "I've had a terrible morning. That 'independence' dress of Nogo's has made her very mean, and I don't know what's happened to Matthew. He said his name was Jamba now." He stopped when he saw the look on their faces. "Does that mean that he's left the mission?" he asked.

"I hope not," said his mother. "Let's have an early dinner," she addressed Esther. "The ants spoiled our breakfast. We'll all feel better for eating. Soon Father'll be home and then everything will be all right."

But the afternoon wore on and there was no sign of Mr. Manship. "I'm hot," said Paul. "Can't we open the windows?"

"Anyone who opens a window will hear from me," said Esther. "We keep this place locked up until Mr. Manship comes home."

After a while Ombua stood up and stretched. He went to the door and Esther let him out. "He's lucky," grumbled Paul. But he didn't feel quite easy. "Be careful now," he said to the dog. "Don't get mixed up in any trouble."

They were eating supper when there was a sound of shouts followed by gunshots. "It's Quadros," said Paul. "He said he'd shoot them down like dogs."

"If he does that, he'll start something that won't be stopped in a hurry," said Esther.

45

Mrs. Manship took Paul's hand, but she didn't say anything.

They were still straining their ears when a rush of feet sounded in the courtyard. "It's Yona," said Paul, "and a lot more of them. What are they going to do?"

They clung to each other, but it was all over in a minute. The men had raced across the courtyard and through the back gate without a halt.

"It's a shortcut through the mission yard," said Esther. "They're running away."

Mrs. Manship was drawing the curtains. "We don't want to see anyone else," she stated.

Paul sniffed. "I smell smoke."

His mother nodded. "I'm afraid they fired Mr. Quadros' cotton again."

They had no appetite for supper. "Shall I read a little?" Mrs. Manship took down a book, but it was no use. They couldn't listen. After a while she gave up, and they sat listening to distant shouts, sniffing the air that was laden with smoke. When the sound of drums began again they could no longer pretend that all was well. They huddled close together and waited for whatever might come.

A tap sounded at the kitchen door. They sat tense and unmoving, but it came again. "It's Daniel. Let me in." The voice was soft. He came in with a finger on his lip. "The Quadros plantation is all ablaze and so is his house. There's no hope of putting the fire out. He says the missionaries have put the rebels up to it. He's got a lot of white settlers with him and they're going to burn the school. You'll have to get away fast."

"Where can we go?" Mrs. Manship was pale but her voice was steady.

"You can go to the forge for tonight," said Daniel. "Paul knows the way there. Tomorrow I'll take you to Olonji. It's the nearest place with white settlers. You'll be safe there."

"But it's all of twenty-five miles. Couldn't we go to Mr. Von Schein's house until Mr. Manship comes home?"

"He's gone already. They've burned his place too. The whole country is in an uproar, and they say no one in the city is allowed to leave. Mr. Manship won't be able to get away."

Mrs. Manship's mind was made up. "Paul, get some blankets. It'll be cold at the forge. Esther, will you get some food together. Let me see, I'll take the flashlight. We'll need matches and toothbrushes and the first-aid kit." She was collecting things as she talked. Paul and Daniel made a blanket roll and put some things inside. Esther came in with her head basket full of food and the thermos jug of water. The smell of smoke was strong now. There was movement in the courtyard and the sound of muffled voices.

"Let us kneel for a minute," said Mrs. Manship. When they stood up she put out the light.

The lamp was out, but the room was filled with a flickering light. Daniel opened the back door and looked out. The schoolhouse was already in flames. A crowd of white men stood watching as the man Quadros poured on kerosine. They jumped back as the fire shot skyward. The front of the courtyard was bright as day, but in the shadow of the mission house it was dark.

"Make for the back gate," whispered Daniel. "Don't stop for anything. Paul, go to the forge. I'll meet you there."

They were out in the courtyard, Paul and his mother holding tight to each other. Esther, the food basket on her head, was close behind. When a hoarse shout went up from the men, Mrs. Manship faltered, but Esther dragged her on. They were through the gate, stumbling in the high grass, not caring where they were going, only to get away. Vines caught at them; sharp spines slashed their faces. At last they drew up, panting.

"Where's Daniel?" cried Paul.

His mother was staring back the way they had come. The fire had leaped to the mission house and it was in flames now. Ten years of work all gone in minutes, she thought. Esther was crying.

Tears wouldn't help. "Which way do we go, Paul?" asked Mrs. Manship. "We may as well go on. Daniel must have lost us somewhere, but he said he'd meet us at the forge. The best thing for us to do is to go there."

Paul started in a fright. He was the only one who had ever been to the forge. Everything depended on him, and he had no idea which way to go. The fire and smoke and the shouting were behind them, but all around was the African dark. He knew that wild beasts as terrible as the men they had fled from prowled there. Even

50

now something was coming through the grass. He stood paralyzed. Then a cold nose touched his hand. Ombua. Daniel had said Ombua would help him find the forge, and Ombua had come just when he was most needed. With the dog beside him, Paul felt calm. The moon was coming up, and objects around them began to take shape. Far away a tree was outlined against the sky. "The takula tree," said Paul. "I know the way now."

At the door of the forge he hesitated. It was pitch dark inside. He didn't want to go in. "This is where the flashlight comes in handy," his mother spoke behind him. The beam lighted the little place. "Why, it's very nice," she said. "There're even benches to sit on." When they were settled she turned off the light. "We must save the battery," she explained. "We may need it later."

They sat in the dark, cold and wet from the high grass, huddled miserably together, wrapped in the blankets. Paul was terribly tired. "I wish Daniel's mother's brother had left a bed," he said.

"We could cut elephant grass and make beds," said Esther. "I have a bush knife."

They went out together. The moon was high, and there was plenty of light to cut the grass. They came back with their arms full.

"If we go to sleep, will we hear Daniel when he comes in?" asked Paul.

51

Esther sighed. "I'm scared for fear those white men have caught him."

"Oh, no," cried Paul.

"We won't even think such things," said his mother. "There are all sorts of good reasons why he hasn't come yet. Anyway, if they did catch him, Daniel is a very smart boy. He can explain what he was doing there. Surely even the worst white settler wouldn't want us to come to harm. Daniel isn't like so many poor fellows who don't understand the language. Daniel can speak for himself. Now we'd better lie down and get some rest. It's a long walk to Olonji, and we want to be fresh and ready to start when Daniel says to."

The bed was hard. We should have cut more elephant grass, thought Paul. He was sure he couldn't sleep a wink. But it was broad daylight when he opened his eyes.

"Has Daniel come?" he asked, sitting up with a start.

"Not yet." His mother tried to speak cheerfully, but she couldn't quite keep the uneasiness out of her voice.

"Oh, where is he?" cried Paul.

"We certainly aren't going to give up about him," said his mother. "And Esther has breakfast ready for us."

There was a fire in the fire pit. Sweet potatoes and antelope meat were heating on the charcoal. A saucepan of water was almost on the boil. "I brought instant coffee," Esther announced proudly.

"It's like another picnic," said Mrs. Manship.

They were still worried, there was no doubt about it, but the food helped.

"It's a good place to hide," said Esther.

"That's what Daniel said. I wish he'd come," said Paul.

"So do we all," his mother told him, "but the soldiers will surely be arriving soon to settle the troubles. Then your father will come, and pretty soon everything will be all right again."

But how can things be all right again? thought Paul. He remembered the look on Yona's cruel face when he had shouted, *White ant, get out,* and the hatred in Quadros' voice when he had said the missionaries were to blame for the uprising. He could still see Quadros pouring kerosine on the mission fire and hear the shouts of the men who had been their neighbors. Here they were, two women and a boy, hated by both sides, and caught between mobs of angry men. The happy, carefree life he had known was suddenly gone. And worst of all, where was Daniel? He opened his mouth to say this, but something stopped him. His mother wasn't complaining and neither was Esther. Brace up, he told himself.

"Sure," he heard himself saying. "Father'll settle that Quadros. He'll make him build a new mission for us. They'll send Yona back

53

where he came from. And Daniel—" he had to stop to swallow— "Daniel will be coming along soon, I guess," he ended a little lamely. His mother and Esther were smiling. He had said the right thing after all.

Chapter

4

"I THINK I'd better go out and look around," suggested Esther after a while. "Maybe I can find someone who'll tell me what's going on."

"I'll go too," Paul announced. "I want to find Daniel."

"No. It wouldn't be safe for a white boy," Esther told him.

"But is it safe for you?" asked Mrs. Manship.

"Who would pay any attention to me?" laughed Esther. "I don't amount to anything."

"You do too," cried Paul.

"I should say so," said his mother.

Esther smiled. "I'll get some water," she said, picking up the thermos jug. "You stay right here no matter how long I'm gone. This is the safest place for you."

"Ombua," ordered Paul, "go along with Esther. Take care of her."

Girl and dog started off together, and Paul

and his mother sat down to wait. "What if Daniel never comes?" asked Paul.

"We won't even think of such a thing," said his mother. "He'll come, all right. All we have to do is to stay right here. Esther says it's a safe place, and Daniel said the news of the troubles had reached the city. Probably soldiers are already on the way here. Things will soon be all right again."

"How would Daniel know what was going on in the city?" Paul wondered.

"Remember the bush telegraph," his mother said. "The Africans don't need our radios and telegraphs. News spreads like wildfire. They always know things before we do."

"If Father comes back home, how'll he know where we are?" Paul worried.

"Esther will tell him."

"And she said she didn't amount to anything," said Paul. "She sure does."

It was a long time before Esther came back. Even Mrs. Manship began to worry. When at last she appeared they greeted her with cries of joy. She had the water, and Ombua had caught a rabbit. But she was very sober. "Things are bad, Mrs. Manship." It was all she would say at first. She fell to skinning the rabbit, then wrapped it in leaves and laid it over the coals to roast.

They waited patiently, but finally Mrs. Manship could keep quiet no longer. "Now," she said, when the rabbit was cooking, "tell us what you found out."

"Everybody's hiding," said Esther, "even the white men. They're scared too. The school's all gone and most of the house. Hymnbooks and schoolbooks lying all about and Ngonga sitting there crying. He doesn't know anything about Daniel. Matthew is off somewhere, probably with Yona. The witch doctor is helping Yona. He's painting the men's faces with white clay. He says it will keep off the white men's bullets. Most of the big houses are burned down, and the white men want to kill every African who has been to school. They say it's education that has made the trouble. They blame the mission for everything. People have all gone crazy."

They sat silent for a little, stunned at the news. "You didn't see anyone but Ngonga?" Paul asked after a little. It didn't seem possible that things were as bad as she said. Then he saw the tears splashing down Esther's face.

Mrs. Manship saw them too. "What is it?" she asked gently.

Esther was crying in earnest now. "Mark Manu was lying in the ditch," she sobbed. "He was all beaten up and bleeding."

"Is he dead?" Mrs. Manship's voice was only a whisper.

Esther shook her head. "I splashed some water on him and he opened his eyes. But he shut them again and lay there groaning."

"We must go and bring him here right away," said Mrs. Manship.

"No," cried Esther, "we can't take care of a man in that bad shape. If we can take care of ourselves, it's all we can do."

"Where is he?"

"In the ditch by the side of the road. It wouldn't be safe for you to go there. Someone would see you. I don't trust anyone, white or African."

"You and Ombua go ahead," said Mrs. Manship. "Tell us when the coast is clear." Paul had the first-aid kit in his hand. They started out, Esther in the lead. It was Ombua who found Mark, a crumpled heap in the grass. He had managed to crawl some distance from the road. His eyes were closed, but he was breathing. Mrs. Manship dropped to her knees beside him.

"His pulse is weak," she said, "but it's quite steady." Paul gave her the first-aid kit, and she tried to revive him. Shortly, he opened his eyes.

"I wanted to warn you," he said, "but Yona —" he drifted off again.

"We can't carry him," said Mrs. Manship. "What will we do?" As if in answer, Mark opened his eyes. "Do you think you can walk if we help you?" she asked. He tried to raise his head. Esther put an arm beneath him. "Lean on us," said Mrs. Manship. Together they got him to his feet. He shuffled painfully along, leaning on the women. Once he almost fell. When they reached the forge he collapsed on the floor.

Mrs. Manship cleansed and bandaged the wound in his head. "It isn't very deep," she said. "He may have a slight concussion. He'll have to be kept very quiet."

This was a complication they had not looked for. To have a wounded man at the forge was not going to be easy. If they had to move on, what would become of Mark? Esther was thinking of that too.

"It's not going to be safe here much longer," she said. "If Yona found Mark so near here, he'll be finding the forge next."

"We can only hope and pray," said Mrs. Manship.

Ombua, who had been pacing mournfully about, suddenly gave a bark of welcome, and they turned to see Daniel in the doorway. But it was a strange-looking Daniel. His face was gray with weariness, one eye was swollen, his clothes were torn and muddy. "Quadros caught me and locked me up," he said. "I just now got away."

"Good for you," shouted Paul joyfully. "I knew you'd make it. Would you like a drink of water? Or something to eat?"

"We're so thankful that you're safe," said

Mrs. Manship. "Eat something first and tell us all about it."

Daniel was famished. They waited until he had eaten, and then he told his story. "Quadros was throwing kerosine on the fire when we ran out of the house," he said. "It was bright as day. He saw me as I came out after you, and grabbed me. I had my bush knife. I could have killed him, Mrs. Manship," he said, "but I didn't. I pulled away from him and almost got away, but someone hit me over the head and I went down. I don't know much about what happened after that. When I came to, I was locked in some sort of shed. I couldn't move at first. I just lay there on the floor. But after a while things came back to me, and I knew I had to get out of there. I began crawling around, looking for a way to get out. It was pitch dark. I had to feel my way, and there wasn't a hole anywhere big enough for a mouse to get through. The walls came right down to the mud floor and that was packed as hard as rock. But I still had my bush knife. They must have been very excited not to have taken it away. I began to dig. I was so weak I had to stop every few minutes to rest, and then I would think of you alone at the forge and I'd go to work again. It took a long time."

Mrs. Manship touched Daniel's shoulder. "Dear, brave Daniel," she said.

"There was no one around when I got out,"

Daniel went on. "Quadros' house is burned to the ground and most of his cotton is gone. Only this shed was left. I don't know where he is, but I know he's out for blood. And Yona's men will stop at nothing. The mission people are caught in the middle. Both sides blame us. It won't be long before someone finds us here. We'll have to get away. Olonji is the only place where you'll be safe."

"But if we go out, won't we fall into their hands?" asked Mrs. Manship.

"I know my way through the bush," said Daniel. "I think I can lead you safely. What's that?" he broke off as a groan sounded from the shadows.

"It's Mark Manu," said Paul. "Yona beat him up. He's got a concussion."

Daniel went over and looked at Mark. "He can't go with us," he said. "If we leave him behind, what will happen to him?"

Mark opened his eyes. "Don't leave me alone," he whispered.

No one spoke for a moment, then Esther sighed. "I'll stay with him," she offered.

"No, it wouldn't be safe," said Mrs. Manship. "We can't leave you."

"No one is going to hurt me," said Esther. "I can hide Mark if anyone comes."

"Where?" demanded Paul. Esther didn't answer.

62

"What do you think, Daniel?" Mrs. Manship appealed to him.

"I—I—" Daniel swayed a little where he stood, and passed a hand over his eyes.

"You're dead on your feet," cried Mrs. Manship. "You must lie down and rest if you expect to lead us anywhere."

Daniel couldn't say no. He was too far gone to protest. "Perhaps we should all rest," he said. "We must start as soon as the sun goes down and travel all night." He stretched out on the floor by the wall and was asleep in a minute. Paul lay down too. The boys slept while the women talked together in whispers.

"I wanted to go to take care of you," said Esther.

"I know," said Mrs. Manship.

"But it's right that I should stay here. Too many traveling together can't be hidden. And I'm needed here. When Mr. Manship comes I can tell him where you are."

"The soldiers should be here any time," said Mrs. Manship. "I wonder if we need to go."

"Need to go!" cried Esther. "You don't understand. There's hardly a white man's house left standing. Yona and his men are raging like lions and the white settlers are just as bad, if not worse. They hate you as much as they do the Africans. You must get away."

"But what about you?"

"They wouldn't pay attention to a poor woman like me," said Esther.

Mark was tossing and groaning in his sleep. "He has a fever," said Mrs. Manship. Esther had been steeping some leaves into a tea. She managed to get a little down Mark's throat and it seemed to quiet him. The hours dragged on until at last the sun went down. Daniel sat up, wide awake, and Mrs. Manship woke Paul.

They ate hurriedly. Esther had made up a food parcel which Mrs. Manship carried. Paul had the blanket roll. Daniel had the thermos jug slung over his shoulder and the bush knife in his belt. "I think Ombua had better stay with you," said Mrs. Manship.

Esther was firm. "You may need him. We are quite safe here." She stood in the door, watching until they were out of sight.

Daniel walked ahead, Paul and his mother followed, and Ombua brought up the rear. Paul could feel his mother's hand quiver in his and he held it tight. For some reason his teeth were chattering, though he wasn't cold. The dark had fallen with the setting of the sun, but Daniel seemed to know exactly where he was going, taking shortcuts through the bush. They slipped and stumbled after him. Once they floundered knee-deep in a puddle. Daniel turned to help them, then he plodded on again. It seemed they could never take another step through the tangle of undergrowth, and yet

64

they went on and on. Suddenly they came to an open space. It was warm beneath their feet. Tiny flames winked in and out, in a burned-over field. The moon was rising and by its light they could see the smoking ruins of a house. Daniel turned aside, skirting a thicket, and almost collided with a dark shape.

"Somebody left his car," cried Paul.

"This must be Mr. Von Schein's place," said his mother. "I suppose he was taken by surprise and had to run without a chance to get the car. But how wonderful. We can drive to Olonji."

"Will Mr. Von Schein make a fuss?" asked Daniel. He knew only too well how a white man could act.

"It will be all right," said Mrs. Manship. "He ought to be happy to get his car back when it might have been burned along with the house. Hop in, everyone," she cried, her voice cheerful and strong.

Paul and Daniel climbed into the back seat and Ombua jumped up beside Mrs. Manship.

"Hold on," Mrs. Manship called gaily and started the motor. "This is better than walking." She headed for the road.

The going was terrible. Whole sections of the road had been washed away by the rains. There were great potholes and ruts so deep that the bottom of the car scraped the middle of the road. The engine roared and sputtered; the car lurched from side to side. "Why would anyone own a fancy car in such country?" said Mrs. Manship. "A jeep is the only thing to drive on these roads." As she spoke the car suddenly turned almost a full circle, then skidded sideways for a few yards. Fighting the wheel, she managed to get it back in the road only to have it sink deep in the ruts and come to a jarring stop.

Daniel climbed out with the flashlight to investigate. "We're hung up on the middle of the road," he said. "The wheels are spinning around. It would take a wrecker to get us off."

Mrs. Manship stared ahead for a minute before she said anything, but when she spoke her voice sounded natural. "There's a wood over there," she said. "Let's go in there and get some sleep. We're too tired to go any farther tonight."

"When it gets light we can see what has to be done," Daniel agreed.

Paul didn't say anything. He was beyond talking. When he tried to stand his legs felt like sticks. He took one step and pitched forward head first into the muddy road. A deathly smell of decay filled his nostrils. It was like a bad dream. Daniel hauled him to his feet. "Up you go," he said and helped him up the slippery bank, and reached a hand to Mrs. Manship. Ombua followed them.

"I'll get some wood together and build a fire," said Daniel.

66

Paul helped him gather chips and leaves for kindling. Daniel found a dry log and pushed one end into the fire when it was burning well. "What is always burning and always moving?" he asked.

Paul knew the answer to that riddle. "The log in the fire," he said.

"Good," said Daniel and gave the log a kick that pushed it farther into the blaze. "All we have to do now is keep pushing the log into the fire as it burns," he said cheerfully.

Mrs. Manship spread the blanket on the ground. It was muddy, but they were muddy too. They lay down with their feet to the fire and were asleep in a minute. Paul woke to feel a chill creeping into his very bones. The fire was almost out. Why didn't someone build it up? He raised himself on an elbow and looked about. Daniel was sound asleep. His mother stirred and sighed but she didn't wake. It's up to me, Paul said to himself and dragged himself to his feet. It was no fun collecting kindling in this strange wood. He hated to leave the circle around the dying fire. Ombua raised his head. "Come, boy," whispered Paul, and the dog followed obediently. Bit by bit Paul fed the fire with bark and leaves. When a good blaze sprang up he pushed the log into the heart of it, as he had seen Daniel do. A splendid warmth wrapped him round. With a sigh of relief he lay down and slept.

A strange woman was bending over him. Her face was streaked with mud and her eyes looked sunken in her head. He stared at her a minute. "Mother," he cried, "you look funny."

"So do you," she laughed. "Wake up. Breakfast is ready."

The fire was burning well. "Someone made it up in the night," said Daniel. "I think Paul did."

"It wasn't anything," said Paul, proud all the same.

A heavy fog hung all about them. Dew sparkled on every bush and shrub. Without the fire they would have been miserable. As it was, they huddled over the blaze, eating cold sweet potatoes and peanuts. It was the strangest breakfast Paul had ever eaten. The sun was just coming up, turning the fog to a lovely pink. Doves were calling in the wood.

"Do you know what they are saying?" Paul asked his mother.

When she shook her head he answered for her. "We believe in stealing."

She laughed just as though she were back in her own dining room. "We don't believe in stealing," she mimicked him back again.

"Will the car go this morning?" asked Paul.

Daniel shook his head. "I've been down there looking things over," he said. "It's stuck fast. The only way to get it out of the rut is to lift it. And that we can't do."

68

"Give me a good old jeep any time," said Mrs. Manship. "Fancy cars are no good in this country. I'll have some explaining to do to Mr. Von Schein, but it might have been worse if the car had been burned along with the house. I suppose, Daniel," she went on, "we'd better start walking, hadn't we?"

"I think I'll have a look around first," he told her. "That little knoll over there should give a pretty good view of the country."

"We'll put out the fire while you're gone," said Paul. He started to get up, then gave a startled "Ouch! I feel black and blue all over."

"Did you hear that creaking noise when I stood up?" asked his mother. "It was my bones."

"Like the Tin Woodsman," said Paul. "And we haven't any oil can."

They stamped out the fire and scattered leaves and dirt over the place. It was better that no one should know they had been there. Paul had rolled up the blanket and his mother had wrapped the remains of the food, when they saw Daniel racing toward them.

"There's a crowd of men coming from the north," he said. "I think they're Yona's. We can't get away too fast. Come on." He plunged into the wood.

Paul and his mother and Ombua were close behind. It was uneven country studded with outcroppings of rock. The trees stood close, but

69

there was very little cover. There was no place where they could hide. Daniel, leading the way, stopped short before a wall of rock that stretched away on either side as far as they could see. A heavy mass of shrubbery grew at its base. Vines and shrubs clung to its sides, but it seemed to rise straight into the air, a barrier that could not be crossed.

"Can we hide in the shrubbery?" faltered Mrs. Manship.

"It would be the first place they'd look," said Daniel. "No, we'll have to climb to the top of the rock. If they come after us, I may be able to push them over while you run for it."

"It's almost straight up," said Paul.

Behind them a sound of shouting broke out. "They're nearer than I thought," said Daniel, "and they've gone crazy. Paul, follow me." He took a good grip of Mrs. Manship's hand and threw himself at the rock before them.

Chapter

5

ALTHOUGH Mrs. Manship was no climber, Daniel didn't wait to let her say no. His hand gripped hers and he started to climb. There were roughnesses in the rock that offered footholds, and vines, clinging to the cracks, gave their help. She dared not look back. "Coming, Paul?" she called. When he did not answer she called again. "Paul."

"O.K.," he answered as cheerfully as he could. But it was far from O.K. There was Ombua. What was to be done with him? "Up," commanded Paul and pointed to the rock. Ombua stood still, waving an apologetic tail. Dogs, he seemed to be saying, don't climb. A burst of shouting near at hand spurred Paul to action. He scooped Ombua under one arm and started to climb. At first he was in a panic, clawing at the vines and shrubbery. The sweat poured down his face; his arms and legs were trembling. Halfway up, he slipped and started to slide downward, but a tangle of vines stopped him

72

before he had gone too far. After that he was more careful, testing a vine before he trusted his weight to it. Ombua seemed to understand and helped by keeping quiet. They had almost reached the top when a new burst of shouting, louder and nearer, made him give a nervous wriggle. At the same time the roots of a vine gave way. Boy and dog started a downward slide, but Daniel, reaching over the edge, hauled them to safety.

The top of the rock was covered with a mass of heavy growth. "Lie down," said Daniel. They threw themselves flat, as a crowd of men burst into the road below and swarmed about the abandoned car. Their faces could be plainly seen, streaked with bands of white clay, so that they all looked alike. Only one man, the leader, stood out from the others. Yona was giving orders, and in a minute the men scattered, spreading out through the wood.

"They're looking for us," whispered Paul. His teeth were chattering again and he stuffed his handkerchief into his mouth to stop them.

There was a crashing in the woods, and voices sounded close. They could hear every word.

"There's nobody here." It was Matthew's voice.

"They must have climbed the rock," another said.

"The white woman could never do that," jeered Matthew.

"Someone has climbed," shouted another in excitement. "See, the vine has been torn."

"A leopard," said Matthew.

"That was no leopard," countered another. But they hesitated. There was no one who wished to disturb a leopard.

"If it is a leopard, let Matthew go and find him," a voice taunted.

"I'll go," cried Matthew, but his voice was too eager.

"No," gritted another. "Yona said we were not to let him out of our sight. Matthew stays with us."

"But why stay here?" Matthew asked. "What is the white woman to us? There are still houses and fields of the white men which have not been burned. And there is the white man's car in the road, waiting for us to ride in it. Come on. White ant," he began to sing, "white ant, get out of my way."

The men joined in the song. Matthew's voice rose high in a wild chant. "Keep to the jungle paths," he sang. "We'll keep to the road. May you be safe from harm. White ant, white ant."

The watchers on the top of the rock looked at each other. "Matthew wants to help us," whispered Paul. "He's singing to us." Cautiously, they peered through the undergrowth to where they could see Matthew hedged in on either side by Yona's men. He was a prisoner, but he had put the men off the scent. Yona had climbed

74

into the car and was giving orders. The men crowded around to push. "Oo-yah," they grunted. The car moved; it was out of the rut. Like a beetle with many legs, it progressed slowly along the road until it disappeared from sight.

Mrs. Manship sat up and pushed the hair out of her eyes. Paul drew a deep breath. He was glad that his teeth had stopped chattering.

"Poor Matthew," said Mrs. Manship. "I think he's sorry he listened to Yona."

"He's in bad trouble," Daniel stated. "But he's smart. I think he'll outwit them, yet."

"I'm glad he wanted to help us," said Paul.

All three of them had a feeling of relief. It was a comfort to think that they had a friend in Matthew. The enemy was keeping to the road. For the time, they felt almost safe.

"We'd better get started," said Daniel.

They moved along the top of the rocky ledge that sloped gradually downward, becoming rougher as it went. Great boulders barred the way. Sometimes it seemed that they had come to a dead end, but always Daniel found a way out. The fog had lifted long ago, and they had left the upland breeze behind them. The undergrowth grew heavier. The sun mounted higher and the country began to steam. Daniel took the blanket away from Paul and, making a bundle, put it on his head. They came to another expanse of elephant grass and Daniel went

76

ahead to break the way. On and on. It was all that Paul and his mother could do to put one foot before the other. Every step was an effort. Ombua was feeling it too. He followed meekly, his tongue lolling. They had almost given up hope when the grass gave way to a rolling meadow with trees and low-growing bushes. It was then, just as things were getting better, that Mrs. Manship slipped and fell.

They tried to help her, but she shook her head. "Give me a minute," she gasped. Her face looked small and pale. "It's my ankle," she said and tried to smile.

"There's a good shade tree ahead," said Daniel. "Could you walk that far? It's too hot in the sun."

She tried twice before she could stand. The boys helped her to the tree, where she sank down, trembling. But it was a perfect refuge. The tree spread its branches to the ground and in its shade the grass grew thick.

"We'll stay here until the sun gets lower," said Daniel. He was gentle with Mrs. Manship, trying to make her comfortable. "Don't worry," he said, rolling the blanket and putting it under her foot. "You're very tired. You'll be better after a rest."

Ombua had already settled himself, and the boys stretched out with sighs of relief. Paul was asleep in a moment. He had no idea how long he had slept, when something woke him. Om-

77

bua, his hackles rising, stared straight before him while Daniel crouched, one hand on the dog, the other grasping his bush knife.

A man's voice was raised in a wild shout:

"White ant, white ant,
   I have driven you away.
   I have driven you away.
   I, Yona, have done it.
   Your fields are burned and so is your house.
   I have brushed you from my path.
   White ant, you who crawl along, get out of my
      way.
   Get out!"

"White ant, white ant," other voices joined in the shout.

Men were crossing the field, walking in single file. Yona was in the lead, waving his bush knife. Under the tree no one moved. They scarcely breathed. The men were so close that each face, made hideous by white clay, was plainly seen. There was Matthew, stumbling unhappily, his arm in the grasp of a man whose bush knife already pricked his skin. The line moved on, the men looking neither to the right nor to the left. "White ant," the voices grew fainter. They were gone.

"What are they going to do now?" asked Paul in a whisper.

"I think they may be going home," Daniel explained. "They've been raiding a day and a

78

night. They must be tired. They'll want to sleep."

"They won't come back here?"

"I don't think so," said Daniel. "Probably the car gave out and they left it. The road can't be so far away. Now that we know Yona's left it, we could chance taking to it. It'll be easier." He looked anxiously at Mrs. Manship.

She tried to smile. "You're the leader," she said. "Whatever you say goes."

Daniel got to his feet. "I'm going to scout around," he said. "You stay here and rest." He slipped away.

Mrs. Manship examined her ankle. It was badly swollen. "It ought to be bandaged," declared Paul. The first-aid kit was back at the forge, but Paul wrapped his handkerchief around it, tying a hard knot over the instep.

"That feels much better," his mother told him.

There was a crashing in the undergrowth. "Baa, baa," sounded a complaining cry, and Daniel came in sight, leading a goat by a stout strand of vine.

"I found her beside the road," he announced joyfully. "She was wandering around all by herself. Probably she came from some place that was burned out. Now we can have a drink of milk."

"But who will milk her?" asked Paul.

"I will," said Daniel. The goat stood docile

while he milked her into the top of the thermos jug, spilling only a little in the process. They took turns drinking. The milk was warm and it had a queer, rank taste and smell, but they could feel new strength with every swallow.

"There wasn't a soul on the road," said Daniel. "It's as safe a time as it'll ever be to take to the road. Are you ready?"

"Daniel," said Mrs. Manship. Her tone was sober. The two boys looked at her in alarm. "I'm afraid you'll have to leave me behind."

"Mother, we'll help you every step," cried Paul. But even while he was saying the words the truth came to him. His mother could never walk to Olonji.

"You see," Mrs. Manship was saying, "my foot is too swollen to get my shoe on. I can't go barefoot." She tried to smile. "You boys go on and get help."

"And leave you here alone!" cried Paul.

"Paul will stay with you," said Daniel. "I'll go alone, traveling fast."

"Dear Daniel," Mrs. Manship's voice was gentle. "No one would listen to you. You know when there's trouble the Government asks no questions. They just clap Africans in jail."

Daniel was silent. He know only too well that what she said was true. The jails were always full in times of unrest. Innocent or guilty, it didn't seem to matter.

"I'll go by myself," Paul declared. "Daniel

80

can take me to the road and get me started right."

"You'll need Daniel and Daniel will need you," said his mother. "Ombua will stay with me. You'd better start before it gets any later." Her voice was steady. They knew it was the sensible thing to do.

"I'll tie the goat under the baobab tree," said Daniel.

As he moved away, Paul turned to his mother. "I don't want to leave you."

"God has taken care of us so far," Mrs. Manship assured him. "He won't forget us now." She was able to smile a little when the boys started off. "Good luck," she called and waved a hand.

"Take care of her," Paul said to Ombua.

Daniel led the way. Once or twice he slashed a tree trunk with his bush knife. "To help us find the right place when we come back," he explained. He parted a curtain of vines, and there was the road ahead of them, hedged in on either side with the green walls of the jungle. Daniel hacked away two branches, and crossed them for a landmark. Then he stepped into the road. Paul followed, glancing worriedly behind him. His mother was there alone. He could hardly bear to leave her.

"Don't worry," said Daniel, knowing how he felt. "We can move fast on the road. And we're likely to meet the soldiers anytime. They'll surely be coming by now to settle the trouble."

"Do you really think so?"

"Of course," said Daniel. "They probably have roadblocks all along. Perhaps that's one reason Yona left the road."

They were making the best progress they could, but the road was not much better than the open country. Sometimes they walked on the raised center, sometimes on the side, skipping over ruts and mud puddles.

"There's the car in the ditch," said Paul suddenly.

It lay on its side, the fender bashed in. "Not much use to anyone," said Daniel.

They were hungry and thirsty and dead tired. Paul had lost track of time. He felt that he had been plodding on forever. When Daniel stopped he kept right on and blundered into him. "I'm sorry—" he began.

"Get down," Daniel ordered quickly and dragged him to the side of the road.

"White ant!" It was the same old song. They lay in the ditch, half covered with muddy water, as men leaped out of the undergrowth, crossed the road and disappeared. The boys stayed quiet, but at last Daniel ventured to raise his head. The road was empty.

"I smell smoke," said Paul.

Daniel nodded. "They've set another fire." He helped Paul to his feet, and the long march began again. They passed what had once been prosperous farms, now smoking ruins. On and on. Once Daniel found some sugarcane and they chewed on that. When they heard a car behind them they threw themselves down in the grass and waited.

"Come out or I'll shoot," a hoarse voice shouted.

Paul and Daniel scrambled to their feet. Mr. Quadros was glaring at them from bloodshot eyes; a revolver was in his hand. Covered with mud and slime, Paul was not a pretty sight. "Mr. Quadros, I'm Paul Manship," he managed.

Mr. Quadros lowered his gun, but his face was still an angry mask. "The missionary's son," he sneered. "It's men like your father that have caused all the trouble. Well," he added grudgingly, "I suppose I'll have to give you a lift, but not that black with you," he added bitterly.

"Then I won't go," cried Paul.

"Suit yourself," said Mr. Quadros and threw in the clutch.

"It's you that make the trouble," shouted Paul. "And you burned our mission. I saw you." His words were lost. Mr. Quadros had already driven on with an angry clashing of gears.

Daniel was looking unhappy. "If it hadn't been for me, he would have given you a ride."

"I wouldn't ride with him if I had to walk all the way across Africa," Paul cried.

"But your mother."

Paul was stricken. "I forgot," was all he could say.

"If another car comes, I'll go back into the bush," said Daniel. "They'll take a white boy if he's alone."

"I won't leave you."

"Remember your mother," said Daniel. "We'll still be friends," he smiled.

Paul didn't answer. He had never felt so wretched in all his life.

"I never told you the story of the leopard and the hare," said Daniel. "Shall I tell you now?"

"All right," said Paul, scarcely knowing what he said.

"It was this way," began Daniel. "One day a leopard caught a hare and was going to eat it, when the hare said, 'Don't eat me. I have something here in my paw that tastes a lot better.'

"It was honey, and when the leopard had eaten it, he smacked his lips. 'Where can I get some more of this good stuff?' he asked.

" 'Let me go and I'll get you some,' said the hare.

"So the leopard let him go and the hare got together a swarm of bees and put them into a gourd, and then he smeared honey over the top.

" 'Here you are,' he said to the leopard. 'Go into your house and shut the door and then throw the gourd on the floor as hard as you can. I promise that you'll get all you want.'

"The leopard did just as he was told. He went into his house and shut the door. There was no window, so it was very dark. He threw the gourd on the floor and out came a swarm of angry bees. It was so dark that the leopard couldn't find the door. He ran round and round and the bees kept stinging him. At last he came out howling, and the hare, who was hiding behind a tree, laughed out loud. Since then the leopard and the hare keep out of each other's way."

Daniel looked at Paul, hoping that the story had cheered him. But Paul's mind had fastened on only one thing—the leopard. "What if a leopard finds my mother?" he cried.

"There aren't many leopards left around here," said Daniel. "Besides, leopards hunt at night. We'll find help before the sun goes down."

"But there might be one," said Paul.

"Yes," said Daniel soberly. "That's why I tied the goat under the baobab tree a long way from your mother."

The blood seemed to be draining out of Paul's body. "What do you mean?"

"A leopard doesn't like the man smell," said Daniel, "but he likes the goat smell. He would go to the goat every time. Your mother will be all right."

"But the goat gave us milk," faltered Paul.

Daniel heaved a sigh. "Little brother," he said, "when there is trouble we have to do the best we can."

"I know," said Paul. "You're very smart," he went on after a minute. "My father says you're the smartest boy in the whole school."

Daniel's head had been drooping, but now he straightened with a smile. "What you say makes my legs stronger," he said. "And I'll give you some good medicine too. There are *men* who couldn't take what you've been taking." He smiled at Paul.

Chapter

6

THE boys walked on in silence for a little, each taken up with his own thoughts. "Daniel," Paul's voice was anxious, "you're limping. You've hurt yourself."

"I'm limping on purpose," Daniel told him. "It rests the leg muscles. My people learned that a long time ago when they used to go on caravan journeys all the way across Africa."

"Why would they want to do that?" Paul was thinking that he, for one, wouldn't care if he ever went on a tramp again.

"They went to trade," said Daniel. "They traded salt and wire, cloth and beeswax, for cattle. Cattle mean wealth in Africa. There is a saying here that a cow is as good as a man."

"Ho, that's silly."

"Yes," said Daniel, "especially since many people in Africa don't even drink milk."

"White people aren't very sensible either," stated Paul. "Look at that Quadros saying this is white man's country. That's silly too."

"It was our country first," declared Daniel.

Something in his tone made Paul turn to look at him. "You—you don't think Yona is right?" he asked a little uneasily.

"No," said Daniel. "He's wrong and so is Quadros. Your father has taught us that violence won't get people anywhere. There's room enough here for us all. If everyone were like your father and mother, there wouldn't be any trouble."

They had come to a very bad stretch of road that took all their attention. They had just reached firmer ground when Daniel put up his hand. "There's a car coming from the other way. It may be the soldiers from Olonji. I'll leave you here."

"Wait, wait!" cried Paul. But Daniel had already slipped away into the bush and Paul was alone in the middle of the road.

A jeep was coming toward him. Could it be Quadros back again? He stood uncertain, then suddenly he was running. "Dad!" he shouted. "Dad!"

The jeep stopped and Mr. Manship jumped out. "Where's your mother?" he cried.

For a minute Paul couldn't say a word. All he could do was point back the way they had come. Daniel, bursting through the bush, gave the answer.

"She sprained her ankle. We were going for help."

Mr. Manship's arms were about both boys. "How far?" he asked. "Get in. We'll find her."

"It's quite a ways," said Paul, as his father started the car. "We've been walking for hours and hours."

"She's in a good hiding place," said Daniel, "under a tree."

"And there's a goat tied off a ways for leopards," Paul added.

Mr. Manship gave him a queer look and stepped hard on the gas. The jeep plowed through a sea of mud, sending a shower of dirty water over them. But he didn't slow up. "You're sure you can find the place?" he asked.

"I marked it," said Daniel, "and slashed some of the trees."

"Good," said Mr. Manship.

"Quadros and a lot of white men burned the mission," said Paul. "Daniel told us to go to his grandfather's forge and wait for him. We've been walking ever since. If it hadn't been for Daniel, I don't know where we'd be, with both sides against us."

"Thank God for Daniel," said Mr. Manship.

"Have you anything to eat?" asked Paul.

"Feel in my pocket. There are chocolate bars. Save some for your mother."

"Sure," said Paul. The boys ate in silence for a little. Then their story came out in fits and starts as the jeep bounced and jounced over the road. Sometimes they would hit a pothole so

89

hard that their heads would bang against the top of the car. "Hold on," was all Mr. Manship said, keeping his foot pressed down on the gas pedal.

"We were going to Olonji by back ways so as to keep away from Yona's men. They went right by us once, but they didn't see us. Matthew was with them. They're keeping him prisoner. He helped us by singing words to us right in the middle of their song about the white ant."

"Are you watching for the markings?" asked Mr. Manship.

"It can't be far now. Slow down a little," Daniel told him.

The boys were leaning out and looking for fresh marks in the jungle wall that looked so solid and impenetrable on either side. Had they missed it? Paul could feel Daniel tense beside him. "There!" They both saw it at the same time.

Mr. Manship stopped with a jerk. "Lead the way," he said as they tumbled out of the car. They moved fast. Paul was running to keep up. A dog barked. "Ombua," they shouted joyfully.

. . .

Mrs. Manship had been sitting under the tree for hours. Ombua slept, but she could not relax. Her ankle throbbed and every bone in her body ached. Her thoughts milled round and round. Paul and Daniel were only boys. She must have

90

been insane to let them go off alone. What if they ran into some of Yona's men? Or what if the white settlers dragged Daniel off to jail? She knew that it could very well happen. It would have been better if she had kept them with her until she could walk. They could have lived on goat's milk for a while at least. At last she must have dozed off from sheer weariness. When she woke, the sun was low and the thought came to her that she would probably have to spend the night alone. Her courage was very low when Ombua gave a bark and bounded away. In a moment Mr. Manship and the boys came into sight.

"Bill," called Mrs. Manship. "Bill, here I am, under the tree."

They sat, the four of them, with their arms around each other, while Ombua lay with his nose on Paul's foot. They had eaten all the chocolate, and Mrs. Manship and the boys had told their story. It was Mr. Manship's turn.

"How did Joseph stand the trip to the hospital?" asked Mrs. Manship.

"He did very well, though the roads were the worst that I've ever seen. At the hospital they operated right away and he came through with flying colors. Then I tried to get you on the shortwave radio but there was no answer."

"Someone smashed the radio," Paul put in.

"It was one of Yona's men," said Daniel. "They didn't want the alarm to go out."

91

"I didn't like it a bit," continued Mr. Manship, "but I tried to tell myself that the radio had been out of order before this and anyway I'd be heading home in the morning. But by night, reports of burnings and riots began coming in. It was pitch dark and the roads were awful, but I got into the jeep and started for home. I got as far as the outskirts of town and ran into a roadblock. No one was allowed to leave town, they said. I pleaded. I said my wife and boy were all alone. They wouldn't listen. They said they had their orders. Troops were moving out and there was no cause for alarm. Only a few natives stirring up trouble. It would soon be over.

"I tried to believe them. I knew our people were loyal, and I thought even Yona would know we were friends. It never occurred to me that the white settlers would turn against us."

"Quadros said it was all your fault," Paul burst out.

"Yona and his men burned his house and fields," said Daniel. "There's nothing left except the shed he locked me in. He's trying to find someone to blame instead of himself."

Mr. Manship nodded. "By morning," he continued, "the fugitives began coming in with terrible stories. Some of them had saved a few belongings, but many had only the clothes they were wearing. The women were hysterical and the men weren't much better. They were raging

92

mad. I kept looking for you, hoping someone might have brought you. Everyone was unfriendly. They kept saying it was all the fault of the missionaries, who had put ideas into the Africans' heads. They said we were educating them beyond the station they were meant to fill, whatever that might be.

"By this time I was almost beside myself with worry. Troops were going out all the time, transport after transport, but they wouldn't let me leave. I sat in the jeep all day and all that night. Then someone spoke to me in a whisper. It was Evova, Joseph's mother's brother. It wasn't safe for a native to be out in the street with feeling running so high, but he had dared to come. He said he knew I wanted to get home and he would show me a way that the soldiers didn't know about. No one noticed when I started up the jeep with Evova crouched under the seat. It was every man for himself by this time anyway. Evova showed me a single track between two buildings, and after that we crossed some of the roughest country I've ever seen. We came out on the road far beyond the roadblock, and then Evova left me, and I went on with my heart in my mouth, not knowing what to expect. I bypassed Olonji, not wanting to risk being stopped again, and when I got back on the road I saw a dirty scarecrow coming to meet me. I thought at first it was an angel, and then I saw that it was Paul." He broke off with a smile.

They could laugh now that they were together. Nothing seemed quite so terrible.

"It'll soon be dark," remarked Mr. Manship. "It's too far to drive back to Olonji at this time of day. Our house is gone. Daniel, may we stay at the forge?"

Daniel's face was beaming. "Esther is there to take care of Mrs. Manship."

"Let's go." Mr. Manship got to his feet.

"I'm afraid I can't walk—" Mrs. Manship began.

"Daniel and I will make a chair of our four hands," said her husband. "Paul, you carry the blankets."

"What about the nanny goat?" asked Paul. "We can't leave her to the leopard."

"I should say not," agreed his father. "I suppose you have no idea where she came from," he said to Daniel.

"She was wandering down the road," Daniel replied. "She might have come from anywhere."

"Well, she's ours for the time being," said Mr. Manship. "Paul, we'll put her in your charge."

They formed a procession: Mr. Manship and Daniel in the lead, carrying Mrs. Manship seated on their crossed hands. Paul, with the blankets, followed, leading the goat, and Ombua brought up the rear. Three abreast, the leaders cut a swath through the jungle growth, their faces whipped with razor-sharp leaves, their clothes ripped with thorns and briars, their feet entangled in clinging vines.

Paul was having trouble with the goat. She was determined not to go a step. "Baa, baa!" she protested.

"Come on," urged Paul, giving the vine rope a tug. But she stood her ground until Ombua gave her a sharp nip on the ankle, which started her on her way.

At last they reached the road. There was the jeep waiting, and they deposited Mrs. Manship on the front seat. Ombua jumped in the back, but the goat refused to get in. After some coaxing, Daniel picked her up bodily and set her in the back, whereupon she made a dive to get out on the other side. "No, you don't," said Daniel and grabbed her just in time. She whipped around, butting and shoving, but he held her fast.

"Do you want to be left behind for some old leopard?" scolded Paul, putting his arms around the goat's neck while Daniel held her feet.

"She fills this jeep fuller than all Joseph's relations," laughed Mr. Manship, pushing the goat's face out of his way. "Keep her out of my hair if you can," he said and started the engine.

The boys were giggling over the goat, and Mr. Manship turned to his wife.

"Are you all right?" he asked her.

"I'm fine, now we're together," she said.

"Where could you find a braver family?" he said proudly.

The sun was setting and suddenly it was dark. The headlights made only a feeble glow in the blackness. The road was terrible. It was almost impossible to make headway through the ruts and puddles. Sometimes they struck a spot where a whole side of the road had washed away. Then the jeep tilted dangerously, and boys and goat skidded across the floor. "Hold on!" shouted Mr. Manship. The engine roared and the jeep plowed forward until it reached higher ground.

"Good old jeep," said Paul.

"It's the only kind of car for this country," said Mr. Manship.

"We've proved that," agreed his wife.

"Daniel, do you know where we are?" asked Mr. Manship at last.

"It's not much farther," said Daniel. "We can make it from here through the high grass. But, Mr. Manship, I think I'd better go ahead and see how things are. Maybe the soldiers have come, but who knows about Yona? It's better that I should go first to see."

"Will you be all right?" Mrs. Manship's voice was anxious.

"Yes, Mrs. Manship," said Daniel. He slipped away into the darkness and they sat waiting. It was very quiet. Even the goat had stopped struggling. Paul's head felt like lead. He leaned it against the goat's rough coat. A strong, rank smell filled his nostrils, but he was too tired to care. He was asleep in a minute.

The next thing he knew, Daniel was beside him again and they were moving. "Straight ahead," directed Daniel. "The forge is under the takula tree."

"Your eyes are better than mine," said Mr. Manship. "I don't see a takula tree. Tell me if I go wrong."

Ombua gave a joyful bark. "Quiet, boy," whispered Paul.

But there was no need for quiet now. "Here we are," Daniel cried.

A figure came out of the shadows. "Mrs. Manship, dear," Esther greeted them, "back safe, at last."

Mr. Manship carried his wife into the forge and Paul stumbled after them.

"I'll take the nanny goat," Daniel spoke behind him. It was only then that Paul saw that he was still leading the goat.

There was a fire burning in the fire pit and by its light Paul could see Mark, his bandaged head showing white in the darkness. Esther was making crooning noises over Mrs. Manship's foot. "It will be all right now that I'm back with you," said Mrs. Manship.

"How are you, Mark?" Mr. Manship was asking.

"I'm doing all right," said Mark. "Only I'm sorry I couldn't take care of Mrs. Manship and Paul. I wanted to, but Yona got to me first. I've been nothing but trouble," he sighed.

Mr. Manship put a comforting hand on his shoulder.

"Something smells good," said Paul. "I'm starving."

"It's the chicken Nogo brought," Esther explained.

"Nogo?" said Mr. Manship. "The last I saw of her she was cross at us."

"Not anymore," said Esther. "She's sorry she ever saw Yona. When the soldiers came she turned her 'independence' dress inside out. She brought the chicken for you and I put it on to cook. I've been praying for you to come back. I know the Lord answers prayer and so I cooked the chicken to be ready when he answered. Why, Mrs. Manship," she broke off, "you're crying."

"Just for joy," said Mrs. Manship.

When they had eaten they lay around the fire, telling their stories. "That Quadros is worse than Yona," said Esther. "The mission is all burned down."

"It seems almost incredible that they would burn us out," said Mrs. Manship.

"They blame the missionaries for all the trouble, and Yona and his men say 'get out.' I guess people don't like us very much," said Paul.

"Our people do," cried Esther and Mark and Daniel. "We love you!"

"As soon as I get well, we're going to start to build a new school," said Mark. And no one noticed that Mr. Manship said nothing to their plan.

Chapter

7

"IT WAS Yona who attacked you, Mark?"
asked Mr. Manship.

Mark nodded. "It was like this," he said. "I
was going out to look at my traps when I heard
a little drum beating in a thicket and stopped
to see what was going on. There was a clearing
in the middle of the thicket, and the old witch
doctor and Yona were crouching over a dead
chicken. The witch doctor was making magic.
He had a little basket that he was shaking up
and down, and every little while he would stop
and look into it. By and by he took out a small
green snake and held it up.

" 'A snake is a bad sign,' he said. 'It says that
you will be tied up by the white men and put in
jail.'

"That wasn't what Yona wanted him to say.
He grabbed the witch doctor and shook him
back and forth. 'Give me a good omen,' he said.

" 'How can I?' grumbled the witch doctor,

'when the chicken you brought is very small and you have given me only a few eggs?'

"So Yona took a knife out of his pocket and gave it to the witch doctor, and the witch doctor began to shake his basket again. 'Ho,' he said, 'here is the nose of a leopard. That is good. The leopard prowls at night. You must do that and you will drive out the white man.'

"Yona had been listening with his mouth wide open and all of a sudden he choked. 'I swallowed a fly,' he said.

"'A good sign,' the witch doctor told him, and Yona swallowed again.

"'But what about the white man's bullets?' asked Yona.

"'I will paint you and your men with white clay,' said the witch doctor. 'My magic is very strong. The bullets cannot hurt you.'

"I was thinking to myself that these men were crazy and I was going away when the witch doctor said something that stopped me. 'The white woman and her son are alone at the mission,' he said. 'Go and get them before the missionary comes back.'

"When I heard that, I jumped up ready to run away and give the warning. But a twig snapped under my foot and Yona heard it. He was on top of me in a minute. I lost my balance and fell backward over a log and then he hit me. Bang! After that I didn't know anything for a long time. When I opened my eyes some-

102

one seemed to be pounding corn in my head. Thud! Thud! I shut my eyes. After a while I remembered about the witch doctor and I said to myself that I had to go and tell Mrs. Manship. But I couldn't walk. I had to crawl along the ground. I crawled and then I had to stop and rest and then I crawled again, but I didn't seem to get anywhere. At last Mrs. Manship and Esther found me and brought me here and that is the end of my foolish story," he finished with a sigh.

"Not foolish at all, but very brave," said Mr. Manship.

"Esther is the one to tell a story," said Mark.

They turned to Esther, who had been listening quietly, and she took up the tale. "The drums went on all night long and there was shouting and singing and pounding of feet. Men began thrashing about in the high grass. They came nearer and nearer, and all the time Mark lay there not knowing a thing that went on. All I could do was sit and wait, and I almost gave up hope. But after a while the men got tired and went away and maybe I slept. The sun came up and there was Mark, still tossing and not knowing where he was. It wouldn't be long before Yona would find us and I didn't know what to do. I waited for hours and hours and then I heard them coming. They were getting nearer and nearer. I grabbed up a lot of elephant grass and spread it all over Mark, and

103

I put my head basket on my head and stepped out through the door as though I was going to work in the field.

" 'Hi! hi!' a man shouted. It was Yona and he had a crowd of men with him.

" 'What do you mean by disturbing a lady in her home?' I said to him.

" 'This your home?' he asked.

" 'Whose else?' I said.

"He came up and looked in the door. It was dark and he couldn't see Mark, who was covered with the grass. 'Where's your man?' he asked.

" 'Where are all the men?' I snapped.

" 'Working for the white man,' he said, real angry, and he began to shout, 'White ant, get out.' It was so loud that it awakened Mark and he reared right up with an awful groan. All you could see of him was his white bandage in the dark. He looked like a ghost." Esther chuckled a little.

"Yona backed away fast. 'Who's that?' he whispered.

"That gave me an idea. 'It's the spirit of that poor man you killed with an ax,' I said to him. 'He comes prowling around looking for his murderer. Sometimes he's an old leopard that coughs and says, "Where's that Yona that murdered me?" ' You should have seen how Yona backed away. He just about fell over the men that were behind him. In a minute they were all gone and not a word said about white ant either.

"Only when they were gone I was more scared than ever. All I could do was sit down and shake and shake. But Mark was all right. 'What's the matter?' he said, real sensible, and since then he's been getting better all the time. And today Nogo came and brought the chicken and she said the soldiers have come and Yona and his men have taken to the hills. So that is the end of my story."

"What a story!" cried Mr. Manship.

"Esther, you're a wonder," exclaimed Mrs. Manship.

"I should say so," said Mark. The next time that old leopard comes coughing around, you tell him: 'Don't stay around here. Go to the hills and look for Yona.' "

"I don't want the leopard to get my nanny goat," said Paul.

"I'll see that he doesn't," promised Esther, who was beaming at all the praise she had received.

"We can never tell you how we feel," said Mrs. Manship, giving Esther's hand a squeeze.

They talked on and on, but after a while Paul couldn't follow what they were saying. Their voices seemed to go away farther and farther, until he dropped off into a sound sleep.

When he woke up in the morning people were still talking. It seemed that there was no

105

end to the things they had to say. After breakfast Mr. Manship stood up.

"The anvil under the takula tree makes a good garden seat," he said. "Come out for a family counsel."

After a night's rest Mrs. Manship's ankle was much better. She limped only a little. She and Paul sat on the anvil and Mr. Manship knelt in the grass. "The Government has said that conditions aren't safe for women and children," he began. "All of them must leave the country at once. I have made reservations for you to fly to America."

Mrs. Manship was pale. "When?" she asked.

"They'll let us know. Probably the first of the week."

"And you?"

"I'm staying as long as they'll let me."

"I'll stay too," said Paul.

His father smiled at him. "The Government says no."

"How can we get ready to go so soon?" Mrs. Manship's mind was leaping ahead. "We haven't any clothes. Look at me. I'm a sight. And Paul too. We can't travel like this."

"I thought we'd drive into Olonji and do some shopping there. You and Paul can stay in the hotel until we get word that you're to leave."

"It's nice here at the forge," said Paul. "I like

it here better than in the hotel." No one said anything to that. "Can Daniel go with us?" Paul wanted to know after a minute.

"No," said his father. "Daniel will stay with me."

This was worse and worse. The mission and the people who belonged there were all he had ever known. It was terrible to think that they were to go away and leave all that and his father too. "I don't want to go," he cried.

"There are things we have to take sometimes," said his father sadly.

They sat in silence after that, while the tears trickled down their faces.

"Missionary, come!" a woman's voice rose in a wail. Nogo, panting, threw herself at Mr. Manship's feet. "The soldiers are taking Ngonga off to prison. Come and stop them."

Mr. Manship was on his feet. "I'll come," he said. "Daniel," he called, "we may need you to get the whole story." He turned to his wife with a reassuring smile, "It will be all right."

"I'm going too," said Paul. They didn't stop him. Nogo ran beside Mr. Manship. Paul saw that her "independence" dress was turned inside out. The letters were only a blur across the back. Daniel's long legs covered the ground at a great rate. It was hard for Paul to keep up, but they all knew there was no time to be lost. After any disturbance the first thing the soldiers did was to gather up anyone they could lay hands on and cart him off to prison where he might stay for months without a hearing.

The countryside was very quiet. There were no women working in the fields or gliding along the paths with baskets balanced on their heads. There was no sound of laughter and high-pitched voices. Everything was silent and deserted.

When they came to the mission Paul gave a gasp of dismay. The school was in ruins. Broken furniture was piled in heaps; books and papers littered the yard. Only the wing of the mission house was left, its windows broken, one side gaping wide. Mr. Manship scarcely looked at it as he strode along the path to the village. Soldiers were loading the men of the village into waiting trucks while their women stood helpless. The man Quadros was directing arrests.

"Here's the ring leader," he said, pointing to Ngonga.

"Wait a minute," Mr. Manship's voice was sharp. "This man is no agitator. He's my yard man and a deacon in the church."

Quadros was not to be silenced so easily. "He fired my house," he said, "and burned the mission. I saw him with my own eyes."

"What a story," gasped Paul. "You poured kerosine on the mission house. I saw you do it."

"That's right," said Daniel a little timidly.

"Are you going to believe this mission kid

and his black friend before you believe a white settler?" Quadros blustered.

The sergeant in charge looked from one to the other, not knowing whose word to take. When Mr. Manship spoke he turned to him with relief. "This man Quadros did set fire to the mission," he said. "My wife can bear witness to it. You had better put him under arrest before he does something worse. He's dangerous."

"Touch me if you dare," shouted Quadros.

The sergeant shrugged. "I'm here to pick up the native rioters," he said. "If you want to prefer changes, that's up to you."

"You won't find any rioters here," said Mr. Manship. "They have taken to the hills. These men are all law-abiding. Two or three are our graduates who are going off to start bush schools. You haven't a thing against them."

The sergeant seemed convinced. Quadros turned away, and when Mr. Manship had identified each prisoner they were released. "It's the white settlers that need watching now," said Mr. Manship. But the sergeant gave no sign that he had heard. Mr. Manship sighed. It was always that way, he thought.

A hush had fallen on the village. The women and children who had been milling around had melted away. They and their men were nowhere in sight. Even the pigs and goats that

110

usually rooted in the dust had disappeared. Only Vitundo, Matthew's mother, stayed. Now she plucked Mr. Manship's sleeve. "Matthew," she whispered. "I don't know where he is."

Mr. Manship looked unhappy. "He was with Yona," he said, "and Yona, they say, is hiding in the hills."

"But he isn't with Yona. He was sorry he ever listened to him. He ran away. I'm afraid they have him in jail."

"Dad! Dad!" Paul's voice was urgent. "Help!"

Quadros was dragging Daniel toward the soldiers while Paul clung desperately to his friend. "Here's one," shouted Quadros. "This is the fellow I had locked up in my shed, and he got away. He may be a pet of Manship's, but that can't save him now."

"Load him in the truck," ordered the sergeant.

"Arrest him over my dead body," cried Mr. Manship. "This is the boy who saved my wife and son and led them across country to safety when Quadros burned the mission. They might have been killed for all Quadros and his men cared."

The sergeant threw up his hands. "Deliver me from the lot of you," he said. But he signaled his men to release Daniel, who stood breathing hard, scarcely knowing that he was safe now. Quadros stamped away, and Vitundo went

111

back to whispering to Mr. Manship while the soldiers got back into their trucks.

"Fire!" someone shouted. Flames were bursting from the thatch of one of the huts. Ngonga and Nogo rushed out screaming. In a moment the village was in a turmoil as women and children raced for safety.

"Let the whole place burn," sneered Quadros. He was smiling.

Here was something the soldiers could do. In a few minutes the fire was under control, and it was then that Quadros got into his jeep and drove away.

Timidly at first, a woman gave a cackle of derision. There was a chorus of hoots and yells. Men and women put their fingers into their mouths and made the trilling noise of triumph. Then forgetting it all, they crowded around Mr. Manship, touching his hands, his clothes, murmuring words of affection.

"You are back," they cried. "Everything will be well now you are here."

Chattering and laughing, they followed him, but when they reached the mission they fell silent. "Ah," they sighed. "Ah." Mr. Manship's heart was heavy as he picked his way through the ruins. Ten years of labor reduced to this.

Paul and Daniel had climbed over the rubbish to peer into the study wing. "Come back," Mr. Manship called. "It's not safe."

"There's a roof over it," Paul reported. "The

112

windows are broken and there's rubbish on the floor, but it could be cleaned up. We could move in there tonight. It would be better than the hotel."

Mr. Manship shook his head, but Ngonga had heard Paul. "We'll build again," he said. "Fellow Christians, will you help?"

"Yes," they cried. "Yes, we will."

Mr. Manship smiled. "We'll talk about it later," he told them. "But Mrs. Manship and Paul and I have to drive into Olonji to buy some of the necessities we lost in the fire. We'll stay in the hotel over night, but I'll be back soon." He couldn't bring himself to tell them that Paul and his mother were leaving the country. Not just yet, he told himself. Whether they noticed that he had spoken only of his own return he could not tell.

They went with him to the forge. It was not a secret hiding place to them. It was Sunday. They had a little service outdoors and then Mrs. Manship sat on the anvil and told the story of their wanderings, aided by Paul and Daniel. Esther had helped Mark out to join them. They laughed and sang. Their missionaries were back. All would surely be well.

Only Vitundo was sad. "When you get to Olonji look for my boy, Matthew," she begged. "He is young and foolish, but he has learned his lesson. If he's in jail, please get him out and bring him home to me."

Mr. Manship put a hand on her shoulder. "I'll do the best I can," he promised. But in his heart he hadn't much hope. Today he had succeeded in rescuing the men from prison, but he knew his influence was getting less and less. The white settlers had made up their minds that the missionaries were to blame for the uprising. They were determined to get rid of them. There would be more reprisals. Dreadful things would happen. Yona's men would make forays from the hills. Nothing would be safe. I must get Paul and his mother away from here as soon as possible, he thought. Even next week may be too late. Olonji would be safer than here. Yes, they must stay in Olonji until they can fly out. His mind was made up but he couldn't bring himself to break the news. Let them all be happy together a little longer. Time enough to tell them when he came back alone.

Chapter

8

IT WAS too late to make a start that night, but early the next morning everyone was back to see them off.

Mr. Manship looked at his watch. "It's time we were leaving," he said. They stood up reluctantly, but if it had to be, they all wanted to help. Mrs. Manship was lifted into the jeep though she protested that she was quite able to get in by herself. Esther came running with a lunch in case they got hungry. "And the blanket," she added.

"But we won't need a blanket at the hotel," said Mrs. Manship.

"You never can tell," said Esther and put it on the seat.

Ombua jumped in, ready for a ride, but Paul pushed him out.

"Take care of Ombua and the nanny goat," he said. "I'll be seeing you, Daniel."

"Come back to us soon," they called after the departing jeep.

"Let's stay only one night in Olonji," said Mrs. Manship. "I want to be with them as long as I can."

"If violence breaks out again, they can't protect you."

"The soldiers are here," she pointed out.

"The soldiers have a way of turning their backs when the white settlers are up to mischief," said Mr. Manship.

"But surely they'd protect us if it came to a showdown."

Mr. Manship didn't say anything for a minute. "The forge is no place for you to stay," he said then. "It's only good sense to stay at the hotel until we get word that there are places on the plane for you."

"We could fix up the study and stay there," suggested Paul.

His father didn't answer. He was too busy trying to keep the car under control. "The whole country is falling apart," he said. "Look at the roads. There hasn't been a stroke of work done on them since the rains."

"If the Government hired men and paid them proper wages, the work would be done. It makes my blood boil to see women working on the roads. I believe I would almost rather have bad roads." Mrs. Manship broke off with a laugh as the jeep plunged into a rut with such force that their heads banged against the top of the car.

116

"There are a lot of things the Government ought to do differently," said Mr. Manship soberly. "We have tried to go along with them because we knew it was the only way we would be allowed to stay. But it hasn't done any good. Every day more of our missionaries are being deported."

There was a sad little silence. Then Mrs. Manship tried to speak more cheerfully. "Maybe you had better let us out before we get to town and Paul and I will come in as refugees so as not to embarrass you." She looked down at her dress as she spoke. Esther had washed it in the stream, pounding it against the stones. Most of the dirt had washed away, but not the grass stains. And it was a mess of wrinkles because there was no iron to press it. Paul's shirt was pinned together with a safety pin and his shorts were in tatters. "You'll be ashamed of us."

"Wait until you see some of the others," said her husband. "They were a bedraggled lot in the city and they may be even worse in Olonji."

"Will there be any boys?" asked Paul.

His father shook his head. "Most of the women and children left the country at the first breath of trouble. Only the diehards are here, and the women are getting out fast. You won't like some of them," he added, turning to his wife.

"Matthew's mother thinks he's hiding in Olonji somewhere," said Paul.

117

"Either that or he's in prison," remarked his father. "To think he was taken in by Yona! I can't understand it."

"He was the only one of our people. Even Nogo only fell for the 'independence' dress."

"And she wears it inside out now," Paul put in.

"They're good people," said Mr. Manship.

They rounded a bend in the road and drew up as they approached a truck full of soldiers. Their leader nodded as Mr. Manship told their story. "You'll find Olonji crammed with fugitives," he said. "No place to stay for love or money." He continued: "You won't find much sympathy either. They say all this is the fault of you missionaries."

"But that's nonsense," Mr. Manship began.

"I only say what I hear," said the soldier and waved them on.

Soon they were entering the streets of the town. "Is this Olonji?" asked Paul. "Are we here already?"

"Riding in a jeep is different from walking," said his father. "You were doing things the hard way."

There were more soldiers barring the way into town and more questions asked. "Missionaries," growled the leader. "You're not very popular around here." But he let them pass.

Olonji was usually a quiet little backwater, but today it seethed with activity. Disheveled and angry men and women tramped the streets. The road was choked with traffic. There was no place to park in front of the one small hotel.

"I'll let you out here," said Mr. Manship, "and come back as soon as I've found a vacant spot."

Paul and his mother stood in the doorway of the hotel. The lobby was a solid mass of people. Some were hugging strange-shaped bundles, all they had left in the world. Others were empty-handed, having nothing but the clothes they were wearing. All were bitter and complaining. More newcomers pushed their way in, jostling and shoving angrily at those who stood in their way.

"This is an outrage," a woman's voice was raised above the hubbub. "These people are like cattle, no better than the natives." She was a well-dressed woman. She had a hat on her head and a handbag under one arm. "To think a handful of wretched Africans can reduce us to running away. If I were a man, I'd teach them a lesson. This is the white man's country."

"The Africans were here first." Paul spoke before his mother could stop him.

"Mind what you say, young man," snapped the woman. "You could be jailed for less. I suppose you are one of those missionaries who have caused all the trouble." She turned to Mrs. Manship. Paul's mother was hurrying him away. "Don't say anything," she whispered.

"But she's all wrong," protested Paul.

"You will only make trouble for us," said his mother.

"She's as bad as Quadros," fumed Paul, but he said it under his breath.

Mr. Manship had come in. He waved to them above the heads of the crowd and began to make his way to the desk. They had a long wait before he came back to them with a worried frown on his face. "There's only one room left," he said, "and it's being held for the Government official, Fernandez. He hasn't called for it, but they don't dare give it up. He's the kind that throws his weight around. The only thing we can do is—"

"One side, one side," a man pushed past them, elbowing his way through the crowd. "Liza," he called, "I have a room. This way."

The woman with the handbag was following him amid the angry glances of the bystanders. "Why does she rate a room?" asked Paul indignantly.

"She's Mrs. Fernandez," said his father.

"What had we better do?" Mrs. Manship asked her husband.

"I'll bring the jeep around. You can sit in it, at least."

"I'll go with you," said Paul. "I don't like it here." He was a little scared. Until two days ago he had never known a cross word and now everyone seemed to be against him.

120

"I don't like it either," said his mother. "We'll go together."

"But your ankle."

"Better to limp than to stay here," she said.

"That Mrs. Fernandez said I could be put in jail," said Paul when they had gained the street. Mr. Manship listened to the story with a serious face.

"You mustn't argue with anyone," his father told him. "You'll only make more trouble. Remember, it isn't easy for the white settlers either. They and their fathers before them have lived here for years. This is their home too, and they've lost all they had. They're angry and afraid too."

"It's their own fault," persisted Paul. "If they hadn't been so mean—"

"They can't see it," said Mr. Manship. "They blame it all on the missionaries who have been trying to help the native Africans."

"Do they really blame us?" asked Mrs. Manship.

"Yes," said her husband. He didn't tell her of the angry comments that had been made to him in the city, nor of the threats in Olonji, even in the little while it had taken him to park the jeep. Better that they shouldn't know how bitter the feeling was. They had reached the jeep, which was parked at the outskirts of the town. "You sit in the jeep," he told them, "and I'll scout around and see if I can find a room in

121

a private house. There must be somewhere for us to stay."

"I think Madame Marie's Maison is on the next street," said Mrs. Manship. "I can go there and buy some clothes while you're gone. Come on, Paul."

"I'd like to stay here and watch what's going on," said Paul. There were more cars than he had ever dreamed of, and more white people than he had ever seen. But no Negroes at all. Were they all in jail? he wondered. A truckload of soldiers cruised by. More refugees were streaming in. He stared goggle-eyed.

His father understood. "Stay right here until we get back," he said.

Left to himself, Paul watched the passing crowds. It was all very exciting, but he had lost a lot of sleep in the adventures of the past few days. His head felt heavy. The blanket Esther had put in the back seat made a good pillow. He lay back and closed his eyes.

Something was tugging at the blanket. Two big black eyes in a small black face stared into his. A little boy was peering out from under the corner of the blanket. Now he pushed a forked stick under Paul's nose. There was a bit of paper in the cleft. Paul took it out. It was a leaf from one of the mission hymnals.

"Who gave it to you?" he asked. The little boy only stared without a word. Matthew, Paul

122

thought. Matthew must be hiding somewhere. "Where is he?" he whispered.

The boy slid out of the jeep on the side away from the street and signaled Paul to follow, then he scuttled away between two buildings and disappeared. Paul glanced around uneasily. No one was looking his way. They were all taken up with their own troubles. He let himself down from the jeep and dived into the passageway. Behind the building was a large yard full of empty crates and cartons. Everything looked unkempt and deserted. Already the jungle was taking hold. Here and there young trees and sharp-edged plants had sprouted. Beyond the yard the woods started, screened by a curtain of tropical growth. The little boy was nowhere to be seen. As Paul stood uncertain, he saw two eyes peeping out of the greenery and a hand beckoned. He crossed the yard and entered a green haze where the trees stood close together, interlaced with vines and undergrowth. A bird screamed overhead and he stopped in alarm. But the little boy was moving forward and Paul followed. They twisted and turned through the dense wood until they came to the bank of a stream. The little boy stopped and gave the call of the dove twice over.

"We believe in stealing." It was as clear as any dove, and in a minute it was answered from the river. There was a cautious movement and a

face appeared in the bushes. But what a face—
hideous, with markings of white raying out from
the nose and encircling the eyes. Paul started
back in alarm.

"Don't be afraid," the voice was hoarse and
trembling. Matthew scrambled up the bank
and seized Paul by the hand. "Paul, little
brother," he cried, "God has sent you."

At the words, a glow of pride and happiness
swept over Paul. He held Matthew's hand in
his and tried to smile reassuringly. "But you
must wash your face right away," he said
anxiously. "If anyone saw you, they'd put you
in jail."

Paul scooped up some water from the river
and began sloshing it over Matthew's head. It
ran down in muddy rivulets. "We must get it
all off," said Paul. "When it's dry it would show
again." He spoke as though he were the older
one, and Matthew listened with respect.

While they washed, Matthew poured out his
story. "When the soldiers came, Yona took to
the hills, but I managed to get away. I've been
hiding in a cave made by the high water and I
would have starved if it hadn't been for this
little fellow." He put his hand on the small boy's
shoulder. "I've been such a fool," he groaned.
"My mother told me to keep away from Yona,
but I thought I knew better. I wanted to get even
with Quadros and the other whites for the way
they treated us. Yona told me that with my

brains I'd be high up in the Government when independence came. I believed him. Then I found that all they wanted was to burn and plunder and that they had no plans for anything else. I was sick to death of the whole thing, but Yona wouldn't let me go. He kept someone on the watch over me every minute. It was only the soldiers' coming that saved me. But I'm a prisoner here too. There's nothing left for me but jail, unless you can help me." His voice had sunk so low that Paul could scarcely hear him.

"Dad will know what to do," Paul comforted. "I'll tell him. But things aren't so good with us either. Quadros and his men burned the mission and we haven't any place to stay, and everyone is mad at us. They say the missionaries are to blame for things. People have all gone crazy."

"And I'm the craziest of them all," said Matthew. "I don't suppose your father will want to bother with me," he added wistfully, "but he's my only hope. When the little boy told me there was a jeep out there with a boy in it, I felt maybe I still had a chance."

A jeep with a boy in it! Paul came back to earth with a jolt. What would his father and mother say if they came back and found him gone? "I'll have to get back," he said hurriedly. "I'll tell my dad." A thought came to him. "Come to the edge of the wood and wait for us.

It would be too hard to find you back here."

"I'll be at the edge of the wood as soon as it gets dark, and I'll wait there all night if I need to," said Matthew. "Give the call of the dove twice over, and I'll come wherever you are, though I don't deserve help," he added humbly.

It was dreadful to see the proud Matthew sunk so low. "My dad never refused help to anyone," said Paul. He turned to the little boy who had stood silent all this time, his eyes darting from one to the other. "What's your name?" Paul asked.

"Utito," he said, a smile lighting his face.

"Utito, little one," said Matthew. "He's half my size and worth more than two of me."

They went together to the edge of the wood. "Look before you go out," whispered Matthew.

There was no one in sight. Paul sprinted across the cluttered yard and had almost gained the passageway between the buildings when a heavy hand caught him by the shoulder and spun him round. A man had stepped from behind a tall shrub.

"Trespassing on private property," he said, giving Paul a shake.

"I'm very sorry, sir," Paul began.

But with the first word, the man loosed his hold. "Who are you?"

"My name is Paul Manship. My father and mother have the mission school."

"I thought you didn't talk like the young

127

tramps that have been breaking and stealing ever since the troubles began. Missionaries," he said thoughtfully. He looked at Paul a minute. "Where are your parents?" he asked.

"Around somewhere," said Paul. "The mission is burned and we have no place to go. My father is looking for a room for us, and my mother is buying clothes, because we lost everything in the fire."

"And in the meantime you're roving around on your own. Don't you know that's dangerous? There are plenty who would take a pot shot at you and ask no questions. What were you doing here anyway?"

Paul swallowed. What was he to say? Certainly he couldn't say he was with a friend who was hiding in the wood. His eye fell on the pump in the middle of the yard. "I—I was thirsty," he faltered.

"Well," said the man, "I'll never let it be said that I refused water to the thirsty. Get your drink. I'll walk back with you and see your parents."

There was nothing for Paul to do but get his drink, though he was too nervous to know what he was doing. Afterward he followed the man through the passage into the street. "There they are," he cried joyfully as he caught sight of his father and mother.

"Paul, where have you been?" His father's voice was stern.

128

Paul didn't have to explain, for the man was already shaking hands with Mr. Manship. "My name is Henriquez," he said and bowed to Mrs. Manship. "I'm sorry to hear you, too, have been burned out. It's the lot of us all. Did you find a place to stay?"

"There isn't a room to be had in the town," said Mr. Manship.

"I can offer you a bunk in my warehouse," said Mr. Henriquez. "I've been living there myself since the natives burned my house. It's at least a roof over one's head."

"How kind!" cried Mrs. Manship thankfully.

"It's nothing," said Mr. Henriquez with another bow. "You had better bring all your belongings with you," he went on, looking at the numerous boxes and bags that Mrs. Manship had brought from Madame Marie's. "Nothing is safe anymore, neither possessions nor lives. I have been telling your boy that it isn't safe for him to be cruising around alone."

"He was supposed to stay right here while we were gone," said Mr. Manship.

Paul looked uncomfortable. "I'm sorry," he mumbled.

Mr. Henriquez led the way through the passage and the Manships followed, laden with their possessions. At the back of the building he unlocked an iron grill door and led them down a narrow hall to a small room furnished with a desk, a chair, and an old cot.

129

"It opens out," he said, nodding to the cot. "Madame," he bowed, "the chair is for you. The rest of us can sit on the cot."

"But where will you sleep?" asked Mrs. Manship, taking the proffered chair.

"My little daughter and I have quarters in another part of the warehouse. There's plenty of room," he said bitterly. "The coffee harvest is a total loss. The workers simply melted away in the bush. Everything is gone. I'm hanging on, hoping something may turn up."

"Your little daughter?" asked Mrs. Manship.

"It's a crazy situation," he said. "My wife had to go to Lisbon for an operation. It seemed best to keep Isobel here with her nurse who's been with us ever since the child was born. Just as my wife was planning to come back the troubles began. Our place was one of the first to be burned. Trying to escape, the nurse fell and broke both legs. She's in the hospital and I'm left with the child. She's too young to travel alone and it's not safe for her here. I'm almost beside myself with worry. It's a wonder," he turned to Mr. Manship, "that you haven't sent your wife and boy home. This is no place for women and children."

"They're flying out the first of the week," said Mr. Manship. "We're only waiting for seats on the plane."

Mr. Henriquez had brought out a spirit lamp

and was making coffee. "Isobel," he called, "where are you?"

Paul started. Isobel. Could it be the girl at the Quadros place?

"Here, Papa," said a soft voice, and a little girl stood in the doorway. Yes, she was the one, all right. He hadn't even noticed the father that day. It had all been too exciting. But this was the girl. She was tiny, with great dark eyes and thick braids. She made a curtsy to the grown-ups. Mrs. Manship put out a welcoming hand and the child leaned against her for a minute before sitting down on the cot beside Paul.

Mr. Henriquez had found a tin of biscuits. "Youngsters like these things," he said and passed them over. "It's a bad business," he turned back to Mr. Manship. "We planters blame you missionaries. Your educating the Africans has backfired. You're trying to fit them for a place they were never meant for. You're encouraging lawlessness."

"Oh, no," Mr. Manship spoke earnestly. "You have it all wrong. We are trying to educate the people to be intelligent, law-abiding citizens."

"We don't want that," Mr. Henriquez interrupted. "We want obedient servants. You're spoiling them."

"Our people at the mission aren't the ones

who are making the trouble," said Mr. Manship.

"What about this Matthew?" asked Mr. Henriquez. "He was one of your star pupils and now he's a ring leader of the rebels."

"Matthew?" said Mr. Manship in surprise. "He's only a boy. He couldn't be a ring leader. It's true he was led astray, but he is the only one of our people. No one else at the mission is interested except to condemn the uprising. As Christians we are against violence."

Mr. Henriquez was not convinced. "I'd like to get my hands on Matthew," was all he said.

Paul's heart was thumping. He was afraid to look up for fear his secret would be written on his face. He jumped when he felt a sharp poke in his ribs. Isobel, beside him, was looking as demure as ever, though there was a faint pink in her cheeks. "Come on," she whispered and stood up. Paul was anxious to get away. They were out of the door in a minute, unnoticed by the others.

Isobel led the way through the warehouse, which smelled of stale coffee, to a room that had been partitioned off from the main building. "Come in," she said, and stepped inside a tiny cubicle furnished with a cot and a dressing table made out of a packing box with a skimpy cotton cover. "I fixed it myself," she announced proudly.

"It's nice," said Paul. "You ought to see the

132

forge where we've been staying," he added, not to be outdone.

Isobel was used to having her own way. "Your old forge isn't as nice as this," she said with a stamp of her foot.

"You needn't get mad about it," said Paul. "We were really roughing it," he bragged. "We sleep around the hearth and sit outdoors on the anvil under the takula tree."

"You look down on me," she burst out, "because my dress caught on fire. But I know a thing or two. The jungle is right behind my Papa's warehouse and I know who's hiding there."

"You don't know a thing," gasped Paul.

"I do too. I followed Utito, and I know all about the dove call."

"Don't you dare tell," cried Paul.

"I haven't made up my mind," said Isobel. "Papa said he would like to get his hands on Matthew—" she broke off as she heard her father's voice.

"Isobel," he called, coming to meet them, "Mrs. Manship says she'll take you with her when she flies out next week. She'll take you right to your mother. What a lucky chance I ran into young Paul here, looking for a drink of water." He clapped a friendly hand on Paul's shoulder.

Mrs. Manship was smiling. "I've always wanted a little girl," she said as Isobel ran to throw herself in Mrs. Manship's arms.

The two-faced little thing, Paul thought darkly, as he watched her. Acting so sweet and all the time planning to tell on Matthew.

"I know a good many higher-ups," Mr. Henriquez was saying. "I think I can arrange an early flight. I suppose you'll be going right on to the city. I'll keep Isobel with me until the last minute. She won't give you any trouble. She's a good child, though a little out of hand, being on her own," he added.

I should think so, Paul said to himself. When Isobel sat down beside him he whispered, "If you say one word, I'll tell my mother and she won't let you come with us."

She looked worried for a minute, then she stuck out her tongue. He was ready to shake her, but Mr. Henriquez was talking about Matthew again. "They say that you people are hiding Matthew," he said.

Mr. Manship shook his head. "We don't know where the poor boy is."

"And you, Madame?" Mr. Henriquez turned to Mrs. Manship.

"I have no idea," she said.

All the blood seemed to have drained out of Paul's body. Mr. Henriquez would be asking him next. What could he say? Isobel stirred beside him. Would she give the whole thing away? He could feel Mr. Henriquez' eye upon him.

"Poor boy," said Mr. Henriquez in sudden sympathy, "he's as pale as a ghost. Come, Isobel, we've stayed too long. These people need to rest. You must forgive me if I've spoken too plainly. Separated from my wife, worried about my child, my business in ruins, I'm not open-minded anymore."

"Things are very hard," said Mr. Manship.

"We're so grateful for a place to stay," Mrs. Manship told him.

"I'm the one to be grateful," he told them.

"Perhaps we'd better say good-by for now,"

135

said Mr. Manship, "as we'll be leaving early in the morning. We'll be seeing you and this young lady in the city." The men shook hands. "Thank you. Thank you," they said.

The door had just closed when Paul seized his father's hand. "Dad, Mother," he whispered. "Matthew is here. He's hiding in the wood behind the warehouse."

Chapter

9

M ATTHEW is hiding in the woods?" Mr.
Manship repeated.

Paul nodded. "He's in a terrible fix. He's
awfully sorry for everything. We have to help
him."

They listened soberly to his story. "What can
we do?" cried Mrs. Manship. "We can't bring
him here. Mr. Henriquez would turn him over
to the authorities in a minute."

"Couldn't we take him home in the morning?" asked Paul.

Mr. Manship shook his head. "I didn't want
to tell you yet, but it wouldn't be safe for you to
go back. I've made up my mind that the best
thing is to drive straight on to the city in the
morning."

"We can't leave Matthew," cried Paul. "We
must drive him home first."

"But the soldiers—" his mother began.

"We could hide Matthew under the seat."
Paul was pleading now.

137

"The jeep is too open," said his father. "If I'm caught with a stowaway, it would be the very thing they want, proof that I'm aiding the insurrection. At the very least, they'd deport me. You know some of our men are in jail," he added.

"We could pick him up beyond the road-block," Mrs. Manship suggested.

"And we'd roll him in the blanket and pile all the packages from Madame Marie's on top of him," said Paul. "Nobody would know he was there."

Mr. Manship sat thinking. "Poor Matthew," he said at last. "For his sake and for his mother's too, we'll have to risk it. How are we to get in touch with him?"

"He's waiting at the edge of the wood," Paul's voice trembled in eagerness. "When it's dark I'm to give the call of the dove, and he'll come to us."

"It's dark," said his father. "We'd better go."

"Oh, do be careful," whispered Mrs. Manship.

Mr. Manship opened the door and looked out. The hall was empty. Quietly Paul and his father slipped to the outside door. The key was in the lock. Mr. Manship turned it and they stepped out into the dark. Mrs. Manship turned back into the room and closed the door. Her heart was pounding. What would happen if they were caught? Why had she let them go, or

138

if they had to go, why hadn't she gone with them? At least they would have been together if the worst happened. She had to keep busy while she waited. Mr. Henriquez had said the bed opened out. She pulled at it and it moved with a creaking of springs. There was a thin mattress on the top. She spread the blanket over it and sat down to wait. The call of a dove, twice repeated, came to her ears. It sounded very natural. Could Paul have made it? Footsteps sounded in the warehouse beyond the door. Quickly she blew out the lamp. The room was in darkness when a tap sounded. Her heart was thumping again.

"Who is it?" she called softly.

"Only Henriquez," came the answer. "Have you everything you need?"

She opened the door only a crack. "Yes, thank you," she spoke very softly.

He seemed to be trying to see past her into the room. "All asleep?" he asked.

"Tired out," she answered and closed the door. She was trembling. He suspects something, she thought. She listened for retreating footsteps, but she could hear nothing.

．　．　．

Paul and his father were waiting at the edge of the wood. There had been no answer to Paul's dove call. "Maybe you'd better call again," Mr. Manship whispered. There was a movement in the wall of jungle growth in front

139

of them and Matthew reached out a hand to draw them into the wood. In a minute he was kneeling at Mr. Manship's feet.

"Can you forgive me?" he wept. "I was crazy. But I never lifted a hand to burn or steal. They couldn't make me."

Mr. Manship's arms were about him. "Come farther into the wood so that we can talk. We can't stay. Listen carefully. We'll take you home in the morning. Follow the river to beyond the roadblock. There's a bend in the road that cuts off the view. Wait there for us. We'll be along at dawn."

"But it's dangerous for you," said Matthew. "They're looking for me to put me in jail."

"We won't worry about that," said Mr. Manship. "Be waiting for us when we come along." He gave Matthew a heartening squeeze of the hand.

"Cheer up," whispered Paul. "I told you Dad would look after you."

They stepped out into the open and stood listening. Perhaps it was only a trick of the eye, but Paul was sure he saw a movement behind one of the bushes in the yard. "Someone is over there," he whispered.

They strained to see, but there was no other sign. "Probably it was some night animal," said Mr. Manship. They stole across the yard, opened the grill door noiselessly, and in a minute were safe in the dark, little office.

"Oh, I'm so glad," breathed Mrs. Manship. "I've had the fright of my life!" She told them of Mr. Henriquez' visit. "He suspects something," she said.

"At least we got back safely," was all her husband said. But when Paul was asleep his father and mother carried on a whispered conversation. "There was someone in the backyard. Paul knew it too. I think it was Henriquez. I didn't lock the door when we came in, for fear he was still out there and it would be a dead giveaway. We'll have to get out of here with the first light and hope he'll still be asleep. If he thinks we're helping one of the insurgents, we may have a bad time of it."

"He couldn't expect me to take Isobel if he made trouble for you," Mrs. Manship pointed out.

"That's true. I'm sure we're doing right to help Matthew," he continued. "I'm convinced he did no harm to property. He was a prisoner to the rebels. But you can't tell that to the authorities. They'd never believe it."

Paul woke with a start. He was lying across the foot of the bed. His mother had put the chair there to keep him from falling out, but he was cramped and uncomfortable. He lay for a minute, trying to get his bearings. What was that? He raised his head to listen. There it was again. Someone was turning the doorknob ever so gently.

141

"Paul," it was only a whisper.

Isobel, he thought disgustedly. He pulled himself out of bed. "What do you want?" he asked crossly, but remembering to keep his voice down.

"Open the door. I've something to tell you."

A fine time to be talking, he thought. He looked back at the bed. His father and mother were sleeping the sleep of exhaustion. He opened the door quietly and slipped outside.

Moonlight was streaming through the grill and by its light he could see Isobel, wrapped in a bathrobe much too big for her. "Mr. Quadros is out there talking to Papa," she whispered. "Come on," she gave a hitch to the bathrobe and started back through the warehouse. Paul hesitated only a minute before he followed her. The window of her bedroom opened onto the alley where two men were pacing up and down. Kneeling in the window, the children were close enough to hear every word that was said.

"I tell you that missionary is hiding him." It was Quadros' voice.

"Mr. Manship told me himself that he didn't know where Matthew was," said Mr. Henriquez.

"And you believed him!" sneered Quadros.

"I think he's an honorable man."

"When he wants to be, but he's ready to swear night is day for his miserable charges. I tell you he's hiding Matthew in the wood be-

hind here. Why else did he park his jeep over here away from everything? As soon as it's light, you and I will go and smoke the fellow out."

The men were moving farther away. Paul missed Mr. Henriquez' answer. Mr. Quadros was talking when they turned back. "We'll have Manship in jail before night, along with his precious Matthew."

"Count me out on that," said Mr. Henriquez. "His wife's taking my little girl to Lisbon to her mother. It's all right to jail Matthew, but I'll do nothing against the Manships."

Quadros spoke in a voice choked wih rage. "I'll go to the Government. It'll go hard with you when they hear you're conniving to aid criminals. We'll see what the Government has to say to you!"

As the men moved away again Paul got to his feet. "I'd better go and tell my folks," he whispered.

"Get Matthew away as fast as you can," said Isobel.

"Are you for him?" Paul asked.

"Of course," said Isobel. "Who do you think has been feeding him all this time?"

"You?" he asked in surprise.

"Who else?" she asked. "He's given me lots of honey from his bee tree. I guess I can give him something to eat."

"I didn't know," said Paul. "You're a good

kid." He swallowed. "I—I guess I'm glad you're flying to Lisbon with us."

"Me too," she giggled and gave him a push.

Paul's father and mother met him at the door. "What's going on?" Mr. Manship demanded.

They listened while Paul poured out his story. "What shall we do?" cried Mrs. Manship.

"We can't do anything until daylight," said her husband. "We'll leave at the first crack of dawn. They think we're heading for the city. It will give us a small head start before they find out we've gone in the opposite direction. By good luck we may get Matthew home before they catch up with us."

"It's lucky Isobel is on our side," said Paul.

"Poor child," his mother spoke softly. "I'm glad we can take her out of all this."

"I don't mind if we do, either," agreed Paul.

"Now," said Mr. Manship, "we must get what sleep we can."

"I don't think I can sleep," said Paul. But he did. The next thing he knew his mother was gently squeezing his hand. "Time to get up," she whispered.

They closed the folding cot and tidied the room. Mr. Manship left a note of thanks on the desk and they slipped out to find a world enveloped in fog.

145

It was very quiet. Only the doves called sleepily from the woods. It wasn't Matthew, Paul told himself. Matthew would be waiting for them beyond the roadblock. He was shivering with excitement, but he clamped his teeth together hard. No chattering today, he said firmly.

In the cars parked beside the road people lay sprawled in uneasy sleep. Others lay about on the damp grass. There were soldiers on guard at the edge of town.

"Where do you think you're going?" their leader demanded.

"There's no place for us here," explained Mr. Manship. "Our mission has been burned, but we thought we'd go back to see if we could salvage anything before my wife and boy fly out for home."

"Better not," said the man.

"But the soldiers are there."

The man shrugged. "They can't do everything. One of the rebel leaders is still free. One of your crowd—goes by the name of Matthew. He's dangerous. He won't stop at anything, they say."

"I suppose it was Quadros who told you that story. Matthew is only a boy. He isn't any leader. It's Quadros and his gang who are dangerous. They're the ones that burned our mission."

"Is that so?" asked the man. He seemed per-

146

fectly indifferent, prodding the blanket roll in an absentminded way. "It's no place for a woman," he said. "Don't say I didn't warn you." He stepped back and Mr. Manship, raising a hand in salute, drove on.

"He's still watching us," Paul reported. "Boy, it's lucky Matthew wasn't inside the blanket."

"No one cares that Quadros burned our mission," cried Mrs. Manship. "How can they listen to such a villain?"

"He's white," said Mr. Manship.

They had passed the curve in the road and the soldiers were well out of sight. "One hurdle passed," said Mr. Manship.

Matthew was waiting. With a flying leap he made the jeep and rolled under the seat all in one quick motion. "Good work," said Mr. Manship.

Mrs. Manship leaned over to squeeze Matthew's hand. He couldn't say a word. He was too near tears. "I'll cover you," said Paul. But though Matthew made himself small, the blanket wasn't big enough. "I don't know what to do," worried Paul.

Mr. Manship stopped the car. "Take Paul's clothes out of the bag and put them over Matthew's head," said Mrs. Manship, "but leave him room to breathe."

"We could fill the bags with grass and pile them around him," suggested Paul.

"A good idea. Be quick; time is precious. We

want to get Matthew back safely before the alarm goes out."

"I'll take my dress out of the box and spread it over everything," said Mrs. Manship.

They worked quickly. "Nobody would ever guess that Matthew is inside," said Paul proudly, as he viewed the mound under the back seat. "Can you breathe?"

"Sure," Matthew's voice came muffled from beneath the boxes and bags, Paul's shorts and Mrs. Manship's new dress.

They started on. "Oh, oh," said Mr. Manship after a little. "Another roadblock. Don't move, Matthew, whatever happens." He slowed up as a soldier came to meet them. The man listened to the same story.

"Take my word for it, missionary," he said, "there's nothing but trouble for you here. You'd better be leaving with your family."

"Aren't things quiet now you soldiers are here?"

"They won't be for long. The ring leader is still at large. One of your mission-educated too. Name of Matthew. All the settlers are up in arms."

"They burned our mission," said Mr. Manship.

The man came close. "They want to round up all of you and the natives who have been to school and clap you in jail. Better get out, missionary."

148

"Thanks for telling me," said Mr. Manship as he threw in the clutch.

"Don't move, boys," whispered Mrs. Manship.

They drove on in silence. "Whew!" exclaimed Mr. Manship at last, and wiped his face with his handkerchief.

"I think the safest place for Matthew is the old forge," said Mr. Manship as he turned off the road into the high grass. Almost at once they were in a quiet world that seemed shut off from danger. "Matthew, you can come up for air now," he said.

The mound of clothing stirred and Matthew's head came into view. "He can take it," boasted Paul. "He never moved a muscle the whole time."

"You can wait here at the forge, Matthew," said Mr. Manship, "while I get your mother. We must make our plans quickly. The sooner you get away from here the better."

"I don't deserve help," said Matthew, "but wherever I go and whatever I do, I'll never forget what you have taught me at the mission. I'll pass it on. I promise you that."

"That's all I ask," replied Mr. Manship.

"There's the takula tree," said Paul. Ombua came bounding to meet them and the goat gave a baa of welcome. Mark was lying in the grass beneath the tree.

"How are you?" Mr. Manship called out.

149

"Better all the time," Mark began, then stopped when he caught sight of Matthew. "It's not safe around here for Matthew," he said. "They're looking for him to put him in jail."

"I know," said Mr. Manship. "I thought the forge was the safest place just now. Have the soldiers found it yet?"

"Not yet," answered Mark.

Matthew crawled out from under the seat. "I am the prodigal," he said humbly.

"The prodigal returned," said Mr. Manship and put his arm around Matthew's shoulders.

"I'm glad you're back," said Mark.

"Where's Esther?" asked Mrs. Manship.

"She's at the mission. They're all there except me. Esther wouldn't let me go. She said my head needed more rest. Mrs. Manship, you'll see something there that will make you feel good." He smiled mysteriously.

"I'll go right over and get Vitundo," said Mr. Manship. "I don't think I'd better drive. I want to be as inconspicuous as possible."

"I'll go with you," announced Mrs. Manship. "My ankle feels all right," she added as he hesitated.

"I'll stay here," Paul decided.

When they were alone Matthew sat down beside Mark, but his eyes roved anxiously from side to side. "Will they find me here?"

"If anyone comes, we'll hide you the way

150

Esther hid Mark," promised Paul. "Tell him about it, Mark."

Matthew almost forgot his worry as he listened. He could even smile a little at Yona's fright. "He doesn't know anything," he said. "He even believes in the witch doctor's magic. He thought that white clay on his face would keep off the white man's bullets."

"Whatever made you listen to him?" asked Mark.

"I must have been crazy. I hated Quadros and the rest of them for the way they treat us, and when Yona said I was so smart that I would be something big in his new Government, I was fool enough to believe him. Then I found out that not a one of them knew a thing about government and that all they wanted to do was to burn and destroy anything that belonged to the white man. I was sick to death of the whole thing, but they wouldn't let me go. Yona had someone watching me every minute. I think he was planning to kill me, but the soldiers came. Yona and the others ran to the hills, and I ran in the other direction and landed in the white man's town. If it hadn't been for Paul, I'd never have got away."

"Did you burn things when you were with Yona?" asked Mark.

"I never did. They couldn't make me. I tried to help Paul and his mother too. When Yona found a car in the road he sent us into the woods to look for you." He turned to Paul. "I saw where you had climbed to the top of the rock, but I said no white woman could ever climb like that, and then I began to sing their song about the white ant. They were like children. They began to sing too, and started back to the road with me. That was when I sang the part telling you to keep to the jungle trails. Did you understand?"

"Sure we did," answered Paul, "and it made us feel good to think you were still our friend."

"It was the only thing I did right," declared Matthew sadly.

"We all make mistakes," said Mark.

"Everyone is against me now," said Matthew. "I don't know what's to become of me."

"My dad will know what to do," said Paul.

"And your mother is a wise woman," Mark told him. "She'll help."

"If only I had listened to my mother," groaned Matthew.

.   .   .

"How quiet everything is," said Mrs. Manship as they walked through the fields. "How could everything change so fast? Was it only the other day that we had commencement and the picnic? We were all so happy. Now that's all over, and we're going back to America."

Mr. Manship cocked his head to listen. "What's that I hear?" he asked. There was the

152

sound of high-pitched chatter, the shouts of men, the laughter of children.

"Look," cried Mrs. Manship as the mission came into view. The place was swarming with activity. Women were collecting broken furniture; children sorted schoolbooks. Some of the men were nailing boards across the gaping holes in the side of the study wall. Nogo, her "independence" dress turned inside out, was the first to see them.

"Hallelujah!" she gave a shout. "They're back."

Dropping their work, everyone crowded about the Manships. They were all talking at once. "Hymnbooks," they cried. "Chairs, tables. The tip-top." Ngonga's voice boomed out over all the others'. "Missionaries," he shouted, "we are making a home for you. No need to go to a hotel. The study will be ready for you by night."

"Come and see what we have done," said Esther, her face shining with happiness.

"Later, dear friends," said Mr. Manship. "Now we've come to get Vitundo."

Silence fell at his words. They all knew what that meant. There was news of Matthew. But no one asked. It was too dangerous a subject to talk about. They fell back as Vitundo came forward.

"Matthew is safe at the forge," Mr. Manship spoke softly.

Vitundo was trembling. "They're looking for him to put him in jail," she said.

"I know. He'll have to leave the country right away. Get some things together for a journey, a blanket, and some food. You know best what's needed. Come to the forge as soon as you can. And, Vitundo," he added, "I know you'll be glad to hear that Matthew didn't burn or destroy. He stood out against Yona and his men. They were holding him prisoner. It was the coming of the soldiers that gave him a chance to get away."

Vitundo had listened gravely. "I'll be at the forge with everything that is necessary," she said. "My heart thanks you for what you have done. God will bless you."

When Mr. and Mrs. Manship reached the forge again, Ombua came running to meet them, but Matthew was nowhere to be seen. Paul and Mark were sitting together, doing their best to look unconcerned. "Oh, it's you," said Paul in relief. "I might have known it, because Ombua didn't make any fuss. We were afraid it might be the soldiers, so I covered Matthew with grass the way Esther covered Mark in case it was an enemy. It's all right, Matthew," he called. "You can come out. It's my mother and father."

They had only a few minutes to wait before Vitundo came, her head basket piled high with things for Matthew's journey. "Mother," said Matthew humbly, "I'm sorry."

She put her arms around him. "If the burden isn't heavy, they say it's not worthwhile," she said. "This is a heavy burden."

"It's worthwhile," Mr. Manship said. "Matthew will have to leave us, but there's work for him wherever he goes, and we know he can be trusted now. Tell me, Vitundo, where is the best place for him to go?"

Vitundo was an intelligent woman. She had her answer ready. "Many years ago my brother ran away to the North because the Government was drafting men to go to the big water to work, and he would not go. The only way out was to run away. I have heard that he is doing well. Matthew must go to him. Tell him, Matthew, that you are Jamba, the elephant, son of his sister Vitundo. He is bound to help you. You will be Jamba in the north country," she sighed, "but you must never forget that your Christian name is Matthew. When the troubles are over, you will come back to the mission."

"The North is a long way off," said Paul. "Won't the soldiers or the white planters catch him? Or Yona and his men?"

"I'm not afraid," answered Matthew. "In Olonji there were too many white men, I didn't know what to do. But in the bush there are a hundred paths I can take. No one can find me there." He drew a deep breath. "I made a great mistake," he said. "I was trying to hurry independence when no one was ready for it. I will try to make up for it by teaching the children so that when they grow up they will be wiser than I have been."

There was no time to be lost. Matthew was ready with his blanket and food. Mr. Manship gave him a little money. They knelt together for a moment. "God bless you and keep you," they said. Then Matthew slipped away.

Mrs. Manship's arm was about Vitundo's shoulders. "He's a good boy," she said. "He will be a help to his people wherever he goes."

Mr. Manship blew his nose. "Come," he said. "I will drive Mark to the mission. It's only right that he should know what is going on. We'll all have a ride. Now that Matthew is gone, it's just as well for us to come out into the open. We have nothing to hide."

Chapter

10

THEY were greeted at the mission with cries of joy. No one asked about Matthew, but when Mr. Manship nodded his head reassuringly, a sigh of relief went up from everyone. They were especially kind to Vitundo. She was not the only mother whose son had fled the country. They understood her sorrow. Matthew had been wrong and foolish, and he had learned his lesson.

"Come, see what we've done," said Esther after a moment of silence. She led the way to the study and stood back proudly while Mr. and Mrs. Manship and Paul mounted the charred wood ramp that led to the door.

"Why, it's wonderful," cried Mrs. Manship. Mr. Manship's desk stood almost unharmed against the wall just as it always had. On it sat three tomato cans, their labels singed but still readable. The family picture hung above the desk, though its glass was broken. The bookcase still held its rows of books. The floor was swept. Everything was neat and in order.

"See," cried Esther and pointed to the tip-top garbage can beside the desk. There was a dent in it, but when she gently pressed the pedal, the top flew up as briskly as ever.

Tears were streaming down Mrs. Manship's cheeks. She put her arms out as though to embrace them all. They had been fairly holding their breath, but now they burst into happy laughter.

It was Ngonga who finally brought them back to the business in hand. "To the work! To the work!" he cried at last. They scattered, still laughing.

Daniel was beside Paul. "I've been going through the ashes of the schoolhouse," he said. "Come and help me. What about Matthew?" he whispered when Paul had come close.

"He's going to his mother's brother in the north," Paul told him. "Boy, but we've had a time. Matthew was hiding in the woods near Olonji. They're all out to get him and put him in prison. But we brought him back, wrapped in a blanket and my new shorts, and the soldiers never knew it."

"Your father and mother can do anything," said Daniel. "As long as they stay with us we don't have anything to worry about."

Paul drew a long breath. "Mother and I have to go away," he said. "The Government has decided that all women and children must leave the country. I'm not a child exactly, but—"

"You're going away?"

"The first of the week. But don't tell anyone else."

"And your father?"

"He's going to stay as long as they'll let him. But you know they say the missionaries are to blame for the troubles. They say it's our fault for teaching the Africans. They want to get rid of all of us."

Daniel had stopped his work and was staring at Paul. "What will become of us if your father leaves?" he whispered half to himself. "What will become of us?"

"I'm hoping that now that we have a place to stay, maybe we won't have to go after all," said Paul, but his voice wasn't convincing. He looked at Daniel uncertainly. Daniel didn't believe it either. They fell to work in sober silence.

But when everyone was full of happiness and good feeling they couldn't stay gloomy. All day long people worked and when night came the women cooked around the fire. "No antelope," said Esther. "It isn't safe to go out hunting when there are soldiers and rebels everywhere. But we have chickens and rabbits."

They gathered around the fire and, satisfied with good things to eat, began the story of the adventures of the past few days. Ngonga pushed

159

the log farther into the fire and started the tale:

"When the man Joseph was struck with a sickness," he began in a singing voice:

"The white teacher took him to the hospital in the jeep.

"It was far away. Many relatives went with him.

"It was then that Yona, the evil man, rose up to burn and destroy all that belonged to the white men.

"Only the mission was spared.

"When the white men saw this they were more angry than ever,

"They said we were the ones who had been with Yona.

"There was no one to tell them it was a lie.

"They burned the mission.

"The white woman and her son fled, led by the youth, Daniel.

"She ran through the bush with the speed of the antelope.

"Her heart was as the heart of the lioness."

"Her heart was as the heart of the lioness," they repeated the refrain.

"She fell," Ngonga went on. "She could go no farther.

"She sent the youths for help.

"She waited alone, though she knew the leopard might be near.

160

"God led the white teacher to them. They are safe home.

"It is well with us."

"Yes, it is well with us," chanted his listeners.

Now Mark took up the song: "The man, Mark, was walking in the bush.

"He heard the plan of Yona and the witch doctor.

"He thought to warn the mission.

"But they set upon him and left him for dead.

"The young woman, Esther, found him in the grass.

"She and the white woman brought him to the forge.

"He was there without sense or knowledge.

"The young woman stayed with him when the others had gone.

"When Yona came with murder in his heart she put fear into him.

"He ran like a jackal.

"Now," his voice rose in excitement, "the white teacher will marry these two, Esther and Mark.

"And they will live in a hut of their own."

By this time everyone was clapping and swaying in time to the song. "Yes, they will live together in a hut of their own," they chanted.

Song followed song as each story was told and retold. But nothing was said about Matthew. It was not that they were unforgiving, but it was a dangerous secret that must not be told. The singing went on for hours. One by one the children fell asleep where they were. Mr. and Mrs. Manship and Paul slipped away to the study, where beds of elephant grass had been spread for them. Paul was asleep in a minute.

"They are so loving," said Mrs. Manship. "How can I leave them?"

"Things are going to be worse before they get better. Quadros will stop at nothing, and our people can't protect you."

"What have we done that the white settlers should hate us so?" she cried.

"We've tried to educate the Africans."

"The settlers are wicked," she said.

"They are sure they are in the right. They have carved out a place for themselves. They have lived here for generations. Of course, they are angry to see their property destroyed. We have to remember that."

"And what about us?" she cried. "Our mission burned and all our work destroyed!"

"Not destroyed," he told her, "only slowed down. I'm glad about Esther and Mark. We couldn't ask for a better plan. They will be the leaders if I have to go too."

The singing in the yard had stopped. The

sleeping children had been carried home by their parents. The fire had burned to embers. The elephant grass was thick beneath them. In spite of worries they slept.

Paul was the first to wake up. Esther had spent the night with Vitundo, but she was already back. The fire was made and she was stirring something in a pot.

"Are you and Mark really going to get married?" Paul asked as he joined her.

She nodded. "We have to wait until Mark is strong enough to build us a place to live in."

Paul was remembering what Daniel had said about the dew dryer who earned enough money to get married. "Mark will have to earn enough for the bride-price, won't he?"

Esther shook her head. "I haven't a father to pay it to."

"I forgot that."

"Your father has been better to me than any father," Esther said. "I wish he might receive my bride-price."

"Esther," Paul spoke soberly, "did you know that Mother and I have to go away?"

Esther stopped stirring the cooking pot and turned to look at him. "I was afraid the study wasn't big enough," she said. "But we'll soon build on another room. We want everything to be right."

"It isn't that," Paul said. "The study is very

163

nice. But the Government has told my father that all women and children have to leave. They won't let us stay here anymore."

Esther had gone back to stirring the pot, but Paul could see that the tears were streaming down her cheeks. "Don't cry," he said. "We'll be back. You'll see."

"Where are you going?" asked Esther.

"To America. We're to fly out as soon as there are seats on the plane." It came to him then that it was really true. He was going far away from everything he knew. "I don't want to go," he said.

"You'll come back. Promise me you'll come back," said Esther.

"Of course I'll come back," he told her.

"Do I smell breakfast cooking?" Mrs. Manship was in the doorway, pretending not to notice their sober looks. "Dear Esther, always taking care of us."

"You're going away," said Esther.

"We have to go, that is, Paul and I do. The Government says we must."

"And Mr. Manship?"

"He'll stay as long as they will let him. But, Esther, don't let's talk about it now. Let's make plans for today. You're going to be married and we're all happy about that. You and Mark will be able to help everybody. Here is something I bought that I want you to wear for your wedding," she hurried on, not giving Esther a chance to speak. From a pretty box she brought a scarf, which she spread out for Esther to see. It was a soft green, covered over with bright birds and flowers.

"Oh, Mrs. Manship," was all Esther could say.

"Doesn't it look like the jungle at its most beautiful?" asked Mrs. Manship.

Mr. Manship had joined them. They stood together, admiring the scarf. Esther smiled in spite of her sadness.

Breakfast was scarcely over when the workers began streaming back to the mission. They were bubbling with happiness. Their missionaries were with them again. What could go wrong? The buildings were burned, but they would make new ones. They could do anything that was needed.

"Don't tell them that Paul and I are going away," Mrs. Manship whispered to Esther.

"Let them be happy a little longer," said Esther.

The men went back to repairing the study wall. Others started a temporary shelter for the school. Ngonga was mending the chairs that had been buried under a mass of rubbish.

"Daniel and Paul, will you go over the hymnals," said Mr. Manship. "Most of them are torn, but there's mending tissue in my desk."

They were singing as they worked, so absorbed that they did not hear the truck until

165

it drew up in front of the mission compound. Soldiers with machine guns were getting out of it. A short stout man stepped forward importantly. Paul knew him. It was Fernandez, the official from Olonji. Quadros was with him. Paul began to be afraid. The soldiers moved forward in formation, Fernandez and Quadros in the center. They acted as though they expected an attack. Silence fell on the workers. Men and women stood still, and it seemed as though everyone stopped breathing.

Mr. Manship stepped forward with outstretched hand. "What can I do for you?" he asked.

Fernandez ignored the hand. "I demand that you give up the dangerous criminal you are harboring," he said.

"We are harboring no criminal," said Mr. Manship.

"Do you mean to say the criminal Matthew is not here hiding?" cried Fernandez.

"Matthew is not a criminal. He is a boy that was led astray. He is not here. He has left the country."

"With your help," cried Fernandez. "You are aiding criminals. You have a school for terrorists."

"We have had a mission school here for the last ten years," said Mr. Manship. "We have taught the Africans with Christian love, fitting them for leadership of their country in time to come."

"For independence, you mean," accused Fernandez.

"I didn't say that. Surely you can see it's to your advantage to have educated people in your country."

"We don't want them educated. It only makes them dissatisfied in the place where they belong. You are teaching them things with hidden meaning, training them for violence."

"As Christians, we are against violence." Mr. Manship's voice was firm.

Things were going too slowly for Quadros, who pushed forward. "This man brought in a refrigerator full of guns," he cried. "He has a tip-top can with ammunition in it."

"What nonsense," said Mr. Manship. "Where are the guns and the ammunition? You burned the mission. Where have you put them? Produce them if you can."

"You passed them on to the terrorists. They are in the hills, waiting to kill us all."

It was so silly that Mr. Manship could almost have laughed. But Fernandez was in a fury. "Enough of this talk," he cried. "I give you until sundown to leave this place. If you are not gone by then, you will be clapped in jail." He turned and Quadros swaggered after him. The soldiers, with their machine guns, fell in behind them. The truck had roared away before Mr. and Mrs. Manship could collect their senses.

"He's only a petty official," said Mrs. Manship. "You must appeal to the higher-ups."

"There is no appeal," said her husband sadly. "I've been expecting this. Half of our men in the city have been deported. It was bound to happen sooner or later."

The people of the mission had come to life again. They crowded close, their faces full of fear. They had not understood the words, but they had recognized the angry, bullying voice. "What is it?" they cried. "What did he say?"

It was time to break the news. "Dear friends," said Mr. Manship, "we must be gone from here before sundown or go to jail." His voice faltered at their stricken faces. "We are in God's hands."

They were silent for a little, too stunned to speak.

"They have burned our mission. They are driving away our leaders, but we still believe," said Ngonga at last.

"That's so. We believe," they said solemnly.

"There's very little time before we go," said Mr. Manship. "We must make our plans. First, Esther and Mark will be married. Mark will not need to build a new hut. The study is ready for them. They will carry on in our places."

"How can we do that?" faltered Esther.

"God is with you. Remember the Christian
168

teaching. Live quietly, in peace with all men. Quadros will do his worst, but God is stronger than Quadros."

"But Daniel?" Paul's voice was trembling.

"Daniel is too young for the authorities to bother him. I'm leaving my books. Daniel, study well and I hope to bring you to America soon to go to school. There are great things ahead for you."

Paul and Daniel were staring at each other. "I can't remember when there wasn't a mission here," said Daniel. "How can we get along without your father and mother?"

"You will come to America and go to school," said Paul. "When independence comes, you will be ready to help with the Government."

"That is what Yona told Matthew."

"No one is ready for independence yet," said Paul. "But someday they will be. You and I will come back and help."

Daniel took Paul's hand. "It's a promise. We will work together."

"Will you keep Ombua for me?" asked Paul after a minute.

"Of course," said Daniel.

"And what about the nanny goat?" asked Paul.

"Your father will have to decide about that."

They consulted Mr. Manship. "If the owner can be found, the goat must be returned," he told them.

169

"But suppose he can't be?" asked Paul.

"Daniel was the one who found her," said Mr. Manship. "What do you say, Daniel?"

Daniel thought for a minute. "Would it be a good wedding present?" he asked.

Esther was beaming. "If the goat has kids, they shall be Daniel's, to help pay for his education."

"A very good plan," said Mr. Manship.

Three old women were coming through the gate, each carrying a large flat stone. "They have come to build the hearth for the bride," said Daniel. "They have been happily married for many years. They will build happiness into Esther's hearth."

Esther watched with a smile as the old women went to work with an air of importance. Everyone knocked off work for a little while to give advice and approval.

"Where's Mark?" asked Paul. "He ought to be here to see this."

"He's gone to his mother's brother to ask for the bride-price."

"But Esther hasn't a father to give it to," said Paul.

"What about your father?" asked Daniel. "Hasn't he done everything for her?"

Mark's uncle was coming through the gate. There was a folded blanket over his arm and in his hand he was carrying a big ball of wax. At

170

a little distance Mark followed, a sheepish grin on his face. "Here," said the uncle, and pushed the presents into Mr. Manship's hands. "It is a poor thing for such a bride," he mumbled.

Surprised, Mr. Manship hesitated a moment, but only for a moment. Looking up, he saw the whole company with their eyes fixed on his, waiting. He knew what was expected. "The wax and the blanket are very good," he said, "but for such a bride—" he broke off just as he was expected to do.

Everyone nodded approval. Mark and his uncle were beaming. "A little more can be added," said the uncle and took from Mark a length of bright cloth, which he had been carrying.

"Ah," said Mr. Manship, "this is very good. But, dear friends, I have to go away where these presents cannot be used. I would like to give them now to the bride, if you don't mind." His words were greeted with nods and smiles. They could see he had chosen the sensible thing to do. Esther received the presents with downcast eyes and a timid smile, but Ngonga broke into song.

"Yes," they took up the song—"He does everything well."

Vitundo pressed forward. "I have made a brush of leaves," she said, "to sweep the new hearth. May your fire never go out."

"And I have brought a spoon to stir the food

171

in the cooking pot," said Nogo. "May the bride always be hospitable and feed her husband's family well when they come to visit."

Paul didn't want to be outdone. "What can I give the bride?" he whispered to his mother. They conferred a minute, then he dashed off to the study. He was back in no time with the tip-top garbage can, balanced on his head. "It is a small thing to give such a bride—" he began, but just then the can began to slip. He broke off his speech to clutch at it and Esther made a dive to rescue her magic box. Paul's face was red with embarrassment, but it was all right. Everyone was laughing and clapping. He grinned too. He had thought of the perfect present.

It was time for the wedding. Mrs. Manship draped the scarf over Esther's head for a bridal veil, and Mark and Esther stood together. "What therefore God has joined together, let no man put asunder." The company stood with clasped hands and bowed heads for the blessing.

"Dear friends," said Mr. Manship, "we have to leave you for a little, but we will never forget you."

"And we will never forget you," they cried. They pressed close as the Manships climbed into the jeep. "God bless you," they said again and again.

Daniel was holding Ombua by the collar. "Take good care of him," said Paul. He leaned far out to take Daniel's hand. "I'll come back,"

he promised. The jeep moved away. Paul looked back to see them standing together, their hands upraised in farewell.

"I'll come back!" he shouted. "I'll come back!"

Biography of Elizabeth P. Fleming

ELIZABETH P. FLEMING was born in Morioka, Japan, of missionary parents, the first foreign baby in that region. She came to this country while still young and received her education in the United States.

Mrs. Fleming was graduated from Teachers College, Fredonia, New York, and taught school until her marriage, when she moved to Chicago. She now lives in Oak Park, Illinois. She is a ceramic artist, with a kiln in which she fires her own pieces. She likes to garden, to play the piano, and to sew. Her favorite hobby is designing and embroidering gay animals on squares that she pieces together into picture-book quilts for children in the hospital.

The land of her birth has always held a peculiar charm for her. Her first book, *Gift from the Mikado,* is a true story of her own family's life in Japan. It was chosen as a selection of the Weekly Readers' Children's Book Club. She has since written stories with an American background and one with a setting in Ireland.

175